by Jeanna Kunce
art by Craig Kunce

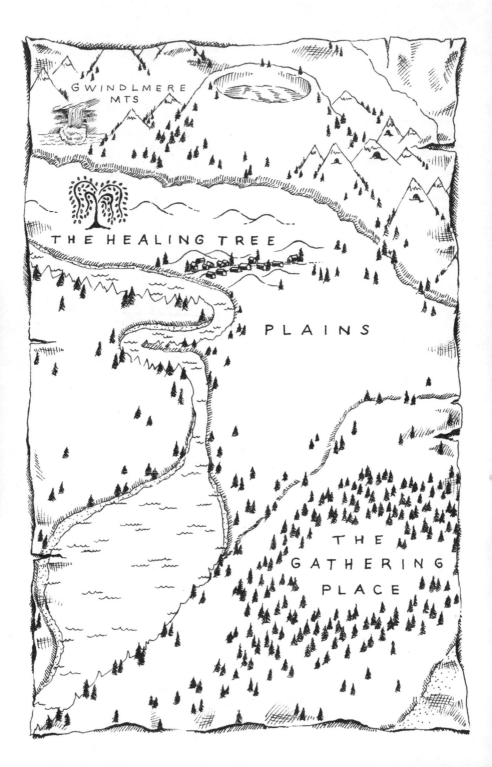

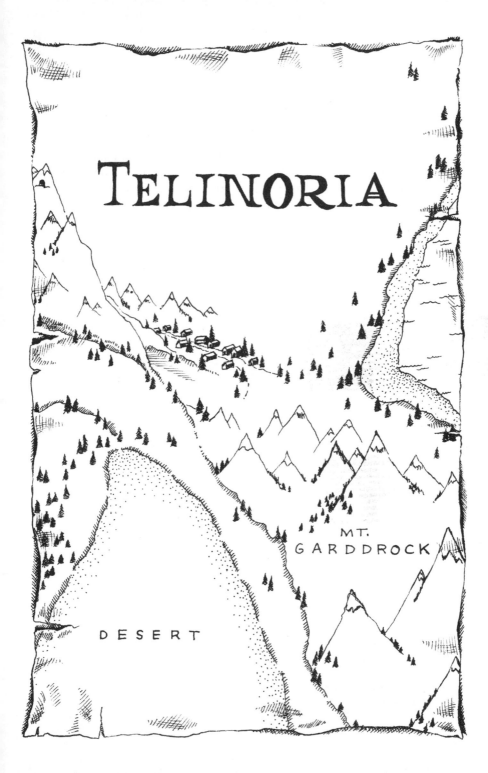

Summary: A young girl named Darien uses magic paints to travel to another world and goes on a quest to rescue dragons from a wicked king.

Published in November, 2014 by Windhill Books LLC, 939 Windhill Street, Onalaska, Wisconsin.

windhillbooks.com

Library of Congress Control Number: 2014938874

ISBN 978-0-9844828-6-3

Printed and bound in the United States of America.
9 8 7 6 5 4 3 2 1

Acknowledgements

Thank you to my amazing husband, Craig—without your support and encouragement none of this would have been possible. Alex and Lauren, thank you for your patience and enthusiasm—you make it all worthwhile.

To my first readers, thanks for your suggestions and honest feedback: Avery Wickham, Baylea Wilk, Heather Swenson, Kristin Luhmann, Beth Ann McManimon and Crew.

Special thanks to Stacy Beatse—your hard work went far beyond my expectations.

My heartfelt appreciation goes to my editor Eleanor Duncan. Without you, this book would be awash in misplaced commas, and readers might never have known what really happened to Darien's shoes.

And to all the writers whose works have crossed my bookshelves—thanks for inspiring me, teaching me, and helping me escape when I needed to.

For
Craig, all the days

and for
Alex and Lauren, my little sparkles

Prologue

In a quiet house on a quiet street, a single soft light glowed in an upstairs window. At precisely eight o'clock in the evening, the light blinked out. It appeared that everyone in the house had retired early and gone to sleep.

But appearances can be deceiving.

One member of the household, the father, had indeed gone to sleep. He sat sprawled out on a worn recliner in the basement living room with the mother, who was watching a television show and trying to ignore the father's snoring. They were a normal couple, doing all the things normal people do: they went to work each day; they paid their bills on time; they kept up their home and yard, just as their neighbors did. They had two cars in their two-car garage—not brand new, yet not old enough to be out of place either. They complained about their bosses, who didn't appreciate them enough; they complained about their relatives, who had taken a tropical vacation instead of visiting

them for the holidays; and occasionally they complained about their daughter, who didn't quite live up to their expectations of how a normal daughter should behave.

As the father snored and the mother tried to relax, the daughter was in her second-story bedroom, pretending to comply with her precisely eight o'clock bedtime. She had turned out her light at the correct time and then jumped under her covers with a flashlight and her new library book. It wasn't her intention to be disobedient—it was only that she was easily caught up in the excitement and adventures she could find in books, adventures that contrasted with the plainness of her real life. She could spend hours daydreaming of herself as the heroine in her favorite stories, burying herself in thick books, and drawing pictures of fantastic places and creatures, which afterward she hid under a box of outgrown clothing in the top of her closet.

The daughter suspected that her parents were disappointed in her, even though they never said as much, but she didn't see the harm in daydreaming. She figured that she would grow out of it someday, just like those old clothes, and become the normal (boring) person her parents wanted her to be.

Tonight none of that bothered her. To her, nothing else existed outside of the story that now captured her attention. She turned page after page until her eyes were dry and it got so stuffy under the sheets that it was hard to breathe. In the late hours of the night, long after her parents had done all their normal things— like brushing their teeth and falling asleep on separate sides of their bed—the daughter's flashlight ran out of power, and she reluctantly closed her eyes.

No Ordinary Neighbor

Darien woke up early on Friday morning, but the day didn't awaken with her. Instead, it kept its head tucked behind dark and threatening storm clouds. Darien nestled her head into her pillow, hoping to go back to sleep, but the grumbling sound of thunder shook her wide awake again and out of bed. It had been an unseasonably chilly summer, so she shivered into her fuzzy ladybug bathrobe and padded downstairs in her stocking feet.

From the hallway, Darien could hear her parents talking in their hushed and hurried morning voices. In the kitchen, her mother was saying, "If that girl doesn't get here soon, I'll be late for work." Darien figured they were talking about Jenny, the teenager who came to look after Darien during summer vacation.

Her father sighed. Darien knew that he couldn't be late either. "She'll be here," he said. Just then, the sky flashed eerily with lightning. Thunder cracked. Darien jumped, startled, and looked down the hall to the back window, where rain had started to wash down in sheets.

Her attention returned to the kitchen as the phone rang and her mother scrambled to answer it. Afraid to go in with all the tension in her parents' voices, Darien leaned against the door frame and tried to hear their conversation.

"Hello? . . . What do you mean, you're not coming? We really need you to stay with Darien. . . . Oh. Really, lightning? Yes. I suppose your family needs you if the barn has been damaged. I'm glad nobody was hurt. Hopefully you can come back next week," Darien's mother said.

Darien heard the clatter of the phone hanging up and waited anxiously to see which of her parents would not be going to work. Her mother usually busied herself with housework when she stayed home. But perhaps today she could be persuaded to bake chocolate-chip cookies in the afternoon if Darien offered to help with the chores. Better still, but less likely, was that her father would stay home. Darien still had the paper sailboat he had once showed her how to make, which she had played with in the bathtub until it eventually got too soggy to float. *Maybe today,* she thought, *we can make two boats, and we can have races and battles, and—*

"—from across the street."

What? What had she suggested? Darien leaned closer to

13

the door.

"Are you serious?" she heard her father reply.

"Of course I am," her mother snapped. Then she sighed heavily. "What choice do we have? Anyway, I can see her on her porch now, plain as day, sitting and rocking in her chair, as usual. I'm sure she won't mind coming over once she hears our dilemma. After all, we are neighbors."

Darien flung the door open and stomped into the kitchen, demanding her parents' attention. "You can't make me stay with her! You can't let old Miss Mildew into our house. Who knows what she'll do to me?"

Her mother turned away and began putting on her raincoat, saying, "Darien, this is no time for your nonsense. Someone has to stay with you while we're at work."

"Well, can't you find someone else? What about Kari's mom? What about Mrs. Meyer?"

"Kari's mother has a part-time job now, and Mrs. Meyer had surgery last week," Darien's mother said and walked out of the kitchen.

Darien's shoulders slumped, and she turned pleading eyes to her father. He peered over his glasses and said, "I don't want you to go letting your imagination run wild like it usually does. Her name is Miss *Mildred*, not 'Mildew,' young lady. And I suggest that you be on your best behavior today. I am sure she is just a harmless old maid, but even they don't take kindly to being called nasty names by impertinent children. Now go upstairs and make yourself presentable before your mother returns. I have to get to work."

With that said, the subject was closed, and he became engrossed in the contents of his briefcase. Darien knew that once her parents had made a decision, no amount of pleading, crying, or tantrum throwing would budge them, so she headed back upstairs to get dressed. Through the window, she could already see her mother on Miss Mildew's porch, wringing her hands and shifting nervously from left foot to right as the older woman looked up from her knitting.

* * *

Darien finished brushing her dark hair, pulled it back using a stretchy headband, and sighed with exasperation at her bangs, which were always determined to go their own way. She slipped a green calico-print dress over her head, tugged white tights on, and stepped into her shoes, bending hastily to fasten the buckles.

"Darien, come downstairs now," her mother called from the front door. Darien hesitated, then decided she might as well get it over with—stalling would only make her mother mad.

Tiptoeing down the stairs, Darien tried to get a glimpse of her unfortunate houseguest, but all she could see was the swish of a long black coat and two angry black shoes with low heels and pointed toes. *Witch's shoes*, she thought.

"Darien, quit dawdling or I'll be late. Come meet our neighbor, who has generously agreed to watch over you today." Her mother chuckled nervously and said something Darien couldn't hear.

When Darien reached the foyer at the bottom of the stairs, her mother briskly took her arm and placed her

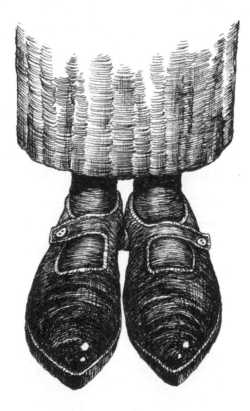

in front of Miss Mildred. At first, Darien could only stare at those black shoes, afraid to look the old woman in the face. But as her mother made the introductions, she risked a glance upward. Because Darien had never seen Miss Mildred up close, she was surprised to find her neither as old or as scary as she had seemed from across the street, although her features were sharp and the set of her mouth was firm. The gray of her straight wool skirt mirrored the silver in her tightly pinned-up hair, while her plain black high-necked sweater accentuated both her slim frame and her hawklike eyes. *She's not so bad.* Darien tried to reassure herself, but at the same time she wished that the woman's eyes did not seem to pierce into her very thoughts.

After mumbling a brief greeting, Darien turned to say goodbye to her mother at the door, glancing warily at Miss Mildred's misshapen handbag as she walked past. Still robed in her coat and hat, her mother grabbed the car keys from the entryway table and hastily kissed Darien on the top of her head.

"Be good," she commanded. "I'll be home before you know it." Darien nodded, hoping to see at least some regret in her mother's eyes, but all she saw underneath her distracted exterior was relief.

Darien watched her mother drive away. Reluctantly, she looked away from the window and toward Miss Mildred, who was standing with her arms folded in front of her chest.

"W-what do you want to do now?" Darien asked, trying to be courageous but feeling more nervous than anything else.

"Well, you might start by taking my coat and finding me a less drafty place to warm up," the old woman stated crossly.

After hanging Miss Mildred's coat on a hook by the door, Darien started to lead the way to the kitchen, then thought better of it. *It might only encourage Miss Mildew to whip up some kind of magic potion if I take her in there.* Instead, they headed down the hall toward the living room.

Abruptly, Miss Mildew stopped and asked Darien to go back for her purse.

Knowing it was a mistake but unable to help herself, Darien argued, "Why don't *you* go get it?" In truth, she was afraid that this seemingly frail and harmless old lady just might be keeping her nastiest tricks in that lumpy bag of hers. Before she could be confronted, Darien hurried through the doorway to the living room, the soft click of low heels close behind.

Miss Mildew's bony fingers brushed Darien's shoulder, making her shudder and flinch away.

"I don't think you heard me, young miss. You wouldn't refuse to bring an old woman her bag, would you?"

Darien retreated further into the room and yelled, "I'm not going near your icky old bag, and you can't make me, y-you witch!" Miss Mildred's eyes did not go wide with shock at these words, but Darien's did. She clapped her hand to her mouth in fear, wishing she could bring the words back and seal them inside. There was no telling what kind of mess she would be in after this; if she survived the day with Miss Mildew, she would still have to face whatever punishment her parents would hand out.

Instead of getting angry, Miss Mildred only shook her head, disappointment clearly on her face.

"I'm sorry for what I said—" Darien began.

"What's done is done," Miss Mildred replied quietly.

"My father said I'm not supposed to be pert-nit, but

I don't even know what that means, so how am I going to know if I'm being it or not? P-please don't put any curses on me; I didn't mean to call you a witch, it just sort of popped out." Darien's eyes filled up with tears, and though she vowed not to bawl in front of the old woman, one hot, salty drop teetered on the edge of her eyelid and slowly tickled its way down her cheek.

The woman's face softened a bit, and she said, "Now, girl, there's no need to cry; no harm's been done. *Impertinent* simply means not having good manners, or in your case, talking of rumors that the other children might have invented without knowing the truth. No matter what you might have heard, I'm not going to turn you into any strange animals or put any curses on you. I'm simply a lonely old crone who doesn't always have as much patience with the wildness of children as she should. It's been so long since I was young myself, after all. . . ." Her voice trailed off, and a strange faraway look came into her eyes. Darien found herself uncomfortably aware that she was becoming curious about this woman, despite her drab clothes and gruff manners.

Miss Mildred seemed to shake herself back from some mysterious past, and she said to Darien, "Well. Now that all that uncomfortable business is over, you may call me Miss Millie, if you like. And as I've not had time to prepare any constructive activities ahead of time, you will have to inform me as to what your days normally consist of." Darien looked puzzled. "Well, what do you do all day, child? Do you read together when that other girl comes? Do you play games of knowledge, practice steps or athletics?"

To Miss Millie's astonishment, Darien burst out giggling. "Jenny? I'm not sure she knows how to read anything except her friends' phone numbers. And considering her weight, I don't think athletics are something she does very often."

Darien ignored the rest of Miss Millie's question because she didn't know what games of knowledge and practicing steps were. "Anyway," she continued, "Jenny hardly notices me in between watching TV, calling her friends, and poking at the red bumps on her face—which she says always show up when she is 'totally stressed out' but that my mother says are from too much junk food." Miss Millie pursed her lips in disapproval but didn't comment on the babysitter's habits. "Most days, I just hang out in my room until lunch. I read a lot. Sometimes I do puzzles. And I really like to draw. Usually Jenny falls asleep in the afternoon, so I can take a turn watching TV, or I go outside if the weather's nice."

"What do you do when you go outside? Perhaps we can find a way to do the same thing indoors," Miss Millie suggested.

Darien's cheeks flushed and her eyes shifted downward to examine the toes of her shoes. "Nothing much," she mumbled.

"Speak up, girl," Miss Millie commanded. "You must do something."

"Well, I imagine things. But you can't tell my parents!" Darien blurted.

Miss Millie's eyebrows rose in surprise and the side of her mouth twitched with the slightest of smiles. "And what do you imagine is so terrible that I can't tell your parents?"

Darien briefly considered whether it was a good idea to confide in this curious old woman, then shrugged it off. "Oh, I imagine all kinds of things, like being other people or going different places. It's not that I pretend anything terrible, it's just the fact that I do it at all that would bother them. My mother says that daydreaming is for foolish and lazy children who won't be able to make it in the real world. She caught me at it once, and I had to spend the rest of the day doing chores to prove that I would be a 'productive member of society' someday. Whatever that means."

Miss Millie looked at Darien for a long moment as if trying to see straight through her. Darien endured the scrutiny as long as she could, until finally she found herself wanting to squirm under the woman's intense gaze. At last, Miss Millie looked up at the ceiling, took a deep breath, then looked back at Darien as if she had made a momentous decision.

"You are so young, yet much has already clouded your mind." She leaned close, and Darien could smell a not-unpleasant mixture of mint and something unfamiliar—flowery, but not common like roses or lilacs. "We've only just met, you and I, but I sense you have an adventurous spirit inside you. I could help you set it free, if only you are willing to put aside what your mother said and trust me."

Miss Millie opened her hands to Darien, palms up, and waited for Darien's response.

"This isn't about drugs, is it?" Darien asked.

Surprise passed over Miss Millie's face, then she chuckled with a pleasant laugh that Darien found quite unlike the witchy cackle she had expected.

"No, nothing like that. But I do have something for you, if you'll only get my bag from the other room. I promise it won't bite you," she added with a huff. "Oh, and tell me where I can find some paper before you go."

Darien pointed to the closet, then she detachedly watched as her feet turned and headed down the hall to fetch Miss Millie's bag. *What am I doing? This is crazy. She is crazy!* At every step, Darien's doubts pounded in her ears, yet at the same time she was helpless to resist wanting to find out more from this enigmatic woman.

Warily, Darien hooked one finger through the bag's drawstring and retreated down the hall, holding the bag at arm's length in front of her.

The first thing she noticed upon her return was that Miss Millie had not grabbed the notebook paper from the closet but the wrapping paper instead. She had taped a four-foot section of it to the wall with the polka-dot-pattern side facing in, leaving the plain white side facing out.

Miss Millie took her bag from Darien's tense finger and casually eased the drawstring open. Darien stared anxiously, hoping and dreading to see the mysterious contents of the large bag, yet it appeared to be pitch black inside. Miss Millie dug around briefly, retrieved one of the mysterious lumps—a skein of maroon yarn with two knitting needles poking out—and tossed it on the recliner.

She reached in again and pulled out a second mystery object: a pair of wire-frame reading glasses.

For the third and final time, Miss Millie searched through the bag's contents and this time removed an item infinitely more interesting to Darien. It was a dark wooden box, about ten inches square on top and maybe four inches high. Carved upon the hinged lid was a slender tree with gracefully curving branches and tiny leaves. Around the four sides were strange markings that might have been merely decorative—or might have meant something to someone who could decipher the symbols. One corner was slightly blackened; otherwise, the box looked old but well cared for.

Miss Millie handed the box to Darien, whose eyes danced with curiosity. With her earlier fears quite left behind, Darien traced a finger over the tree's outline, feeling its smoothly chiseled texture, then gazed eagerly at the delicate latch holding the lid closed.

"Go ahead, open it. It's not locked right now," Miss Millie said, nodding.

Darien held her breath and carefully eased the box open. The first thing she saw on top was a shallow ceramic tray with depressions shaped like half spheres. On the inside of the lid were three paintbrushes, each a different size, held in by silky black ribbons. Darien lifted the tray out and saw that underneath were nine glass bottles of different colors. When she discovered that the bottles were actually clear and only contained ordinary paint, although in an unusual box, she abandoned any further thoughts of Miss Millie being anything except an odd old woman.

"They are concentrated, so you don't need to put much in the tray," Miss Millie explained. "And you can add water as you go along to make them last longer. Be careful not to spill them on you or on the floor." These seemed to be the only instructions she planned to give, as she promptly settled into the rocking chair and became absorbed in her knitting project.

Darien hardly noticed, however, as she was already contemplating the blank paper, her head cocked to the side and her hands on her hips. Without turning away from the paper, Darien said, "I don't know what to paint."

"Remember, use your imagination. Think of places far away, or people, or adventures. Let go. Think of what you would see if your dreams could come alive. Close your eyes and picture it in your head first, if you need to."

So while Miss Millie rocked, Darien closed her eyes, thinking hard. And nothing happened. The only thoughts that came were how foolish her parents would think she was. Very softly, she heard Miss Millie beginning to hum on beat with the rocking chair, and after a while Darien allowed her mind to drift. When she stopped trying so hard, she realized that ideas were coming to her. With the tray of paints and brushes in hand, Darien began to paint.

"What if it's not good?" she asked.

"Oh, I don't think you need to worry about that. Those paints are very, very easy to work with. Just trust yourself and what you see in your head," Miss Millie answered, then resumed humming.

And so Darien began to paint.

A Fall and a Rescue

A bright green leaf started to take shape on the left. The cool, calming blue of a clear lake flowed in from the right. As Darien painted, a scene was appearing almost faster than she could imagine it. It was as if the paints could sense what she wanted to see, and then it became more real and defined than she could even picture in her head. The only sounds were the steady crick-creak of the rocking chair and Miss Millie's hypnotic humming. Darien noticed neither of these; her hands and body moved like she was in a trance. Every time she dipped her brush into the paint, she could feel a shivery tingle move from the brush, through her fingers, and almost halfway up her forearm.

The basic landscape was nearly finished. Sunlight glinted off ripples in the lake; the deep, earthy brown of hard-packed dirt surrounded the water; and every shade of green could be seen in the lush forest filled with plants and trees like no one has ever seen before.

Here and there were small splashes of crimson, peach, and magenta from tropical-looking flowers thriving at the forest's edge.

Darien leaned in closer to add a small flock of gray birds flying in the distance and a soft, brown creature in a tree that looked like a monkey at first glance but was not really a monkey at all. So quickly, the paintbrush moved with graceful strokes here, tiny stipples there, little dabs all around. The colors were so vibrant, the details were so realistic, it was hard to believe it was only a painting. Darien's heart beat faster because she felt the painting was almost complete. The trance-like feeling was fading, and she started to think about what was happening. And as she thought, Darien knew there was one more thing to add, yet she was afraid.

She glanced back at Miss Millie. The woman appeared to have nodded off in the chair, although the haunting melody of her humming still seemed to echo in Darien's head. A warm breeze tickled the hair by her neck. And as Darien turned back to the painting, she thought she saw movement on the far side of the lake. *How could that be? My eyes must be screwed up from staring at the paper for so long.*

Her eyes squinted, and she moved her face up close to the painting in order to see more clearly. *It can't be what I was thinking about*, Darien told herself. But her eyes weren't deceiving her. Something surely was on the

other side of the lake, something she hadn't painted—
and the something was moving almost imperceptibly.
Straining even more to see what it was, Darien leaned
closer. As she took a step, she tripped and fell forward.

In a dizzying flash, Darien fell to her hands and
knees. She struggled to understand why her hands had
landed on a patch of pebbly dirt instead of on the smooth
wood of her parents' living room floor, why a prickly
leaf was tickling her earlobe, and why the thick, musty
smell of a summer thunderstorm had suddenly and

completely disappeared from her nostrils. Before she could even begin to understand what had happened, the silence was abruptly broken by the high-pitched shriek of an animal in pain. Without thinking, Darien jumped to her feet and started making her way through the undergrowth toward the far side of the lake.

Halfway around the curve of the shore, Darien stumbled and had to untangle a vine from her ankle. The rush of the realization of what had happened overwhelmed her. *I fell into the painting. I'm in the painting. I'M IN THE PAINTING! This can't be real. This can't be happening.*

Darien looked back where she had come from. The living room and Miss Millie were gone. In fact, there was nothing but lake and forest as far as her eyes could see.

"Hey!" Darien yelled. "Where am I?" Her voice sounded small and muted in the thick forest. Before she could say anything more, the air was filled again with the animal's terrible cry.

Knowing what she had to do, Darien yanked the vine out of her way and jumped to her feet. She nimbly hopped over small boulders and quickly made it the rest of the way around the lake, despite the thorny plants that clawed at her clothes and bare arms. The crying thing was obscured by a flowering shrub, and she couldn't see the animal until she was almost on top of it. Darien's heart pounded as she stepped into full view of the creature.

The paints had known, through whatever strange magic they held, that what Darien most wanted in her heart was to see a dragon. But this didn't look like any dragon she had ever imagined. First of all, it was relatively small, only about the size of a large dog. Its skin was soft and pink, not green and scaly. The two wings were shriveled and plastered against its body with a syrupy greenish goo. It lay curled on its side in the shade of the shrub, and when Darien arrived, it raised its head and gave a weak version of the cry she had heard from across the lake. Then it looked pleadingly at her as it started to wheeze and pant.

Darien's fear left her, and she knelt by the sick dragon. She spoke soothingly to it and slowly reached out her hand to touch its heaving side. From inches away Darien's fingers could already feel an enormous heat emanating from the dragon's skin. It gave a halfhearted snap of its jaws toward her, but then it lay back and let Darien's hand come to rest on its back. Suddenly it dawned on her that the poor thing had done its best to find a cool spot, but it just wasn't enough.

"You're too hot, aren't you, fella? If I had a way to get some water to you, I could cool you off," Darien said to the creature. She looked around, wondering what she could possibly find that might work.

Nothing seemed to fit what she was looking for. The leaves were either too small, too high, or too fragile. Bark from the nearby trees was papery and thin. Just when Darien thought she could try to cup the water in her hands and bring it over, the dragon moaned once more.

"Well," she said, "if I can't get the water to you, I'll have to get you to the water." Hoping her instincts were right, Darien moved around to the dragon's back and slid her hands underneath its whole body to pick it up. It was heavy, but Darien was just strong enough to carry it over to the clear water of the lake. The hardest part was keeping her hands from slipping in the slimy and, incidentally, smelly fluid from its wings.

The dragon must have sensed that she was trying to help, because it didn't struggle or try to snap at her again. Darien wobbled under the weight of the dragon as she kicked her shoes off and gingerly walked into the water. She felt the firm earth give way to a smooth, rocky bottom. Darien was thankful her feet weren't getting cut to shreds, though her tights were slippery on the rounded stones.

When she was in up to her chest, Darien leaned forward and let the dragon's body sink almost all the way under the surface. Soothed by the cool water, the dragon relaxed its head in the crook of Darien's elbow. Not knowing what to do next, she started to sing to the dragon in a quiet voice. To her surprise, after a while she noticed a gentle vibration as the dragon began to hum softly and tunelessly along with her.

Time passed rather slowly as they soaked and watched wispy white clouds float lazily across the sky. Iridescent dragonflies larger than Darien's head skimmed and dove gracefully over the water, buzzing somnolently, but never coming close enough to seem threatening. Gradually, the intense heat of the dragon diminished. Darien's ankles started to ache from the chill, and she began to wonder how long she would have to remain in the lake with the dragon. Fortunately, it no longer appeared to be in pain at all, and its eyes were becoming more alert to its surroundings.

"Well, little guy," Darien said, "I think we're going to have to get out of the water. My legs are starting to feel numb, and I don't know how much longer I can hold you. Should we see how it goes back on land?" She didn't really expect an answer, yet she was somewhat disappointed that there wasn't at least some sign to tell her what to do.

As Darien waded into the shallower area, the dragon's body slowly emerged from the water. She noticed that its skin no longer looked feverishly pink and had instead started to turn the deep orange-red of maple leaves in autumn. Looking at it in wonder, she took on its full weight again and carried it back into the shade, grateful that all the slimy stuff had been washed away in the lake. Because the dragon still didn't protest, she laid it down and timidly put her hand on its head. The dragon's dark brown eyes stared into Darien's eyes with curiosity.

"It's all right, little one. I'll take care of you," Darien said as she gently touched her fingers over its bumpy head. The dragon responded by blinking its large eyes slowly and making another short hum

in its throat, although it was rather unclear whether the dragon actually understood or if it just liked the soothing sound of Darien's voice.

Abruptly, the bonding between human and dragon was broken by a dark shadow swooping down from overhead. Darien ducked and tried to cover the dragon's head with her body. There was a heavy thump on the ground nearby. Darien turned her head to look while she continued to shield the dragon's body.

Fifteen feet away stood another dragon, this one so large that the top of Darien's head would barely have reached its shoulder. It stretched its dark brown head down toward her, nostrils flaring. Darien shied away from the creature's bony snout and the short, blunt horns jutting from its heavy forehead. It let out a sharp hiss from between its teeth and tried to see the small dragon she protected. For all Darien knew, this new one might try to kill the little one. And though there was probably not much she could do against this big beast if it wanted to attack her, she tried to stand her ground. Her heart pounded wildly as the big dragon took a step closer.

"Leave him alone! I'm not going to let you hurt him!" Darien shouted. She put her hands out in defense when the large dragon hissed again and loomed near. It swung its head into her side, pushing her roughly to the ground. The small dragon loudly squawked in protest. The large dragon glanced over the small one's body, then turned back to Darien, who was trying to get her breath back.

To her surprise, the dragon spoke to her in an oddly accented English, saying, "This dragon isn't a 'him.' She's a baby; I am her brother. And you're the one she needs protection against, Human. Do you think you can just come and steal our hatchlings now too?"

"What? I wasn't trying to steal her. I was just trying to help. She was howling and crying and burning up from fever when I got here, so I cooled her off in the water." Darien scrambled to her feet. "Besides, it's not my fault she was left here all alone and sick," she added indignantly.

The large dragon seemed to roll his eyes. "She wasn't sick; she was just born. The birthing process for dragons is so heat intensive that we need to stay cool for a period of time after hatching. How else will our skin harden and become this strong, protective shell?" At this, the dragon clapped his chest with one muscular foreleg. "And for your information, the only reason we would ever leave a newborn is because our mother was taken right after laying her egg, while she was still weak."

"Taken? Who would take her?"

The dragon's eyes narrowed. "Humans—like you."

Darien Hitches a Ride

Darien was stunned for a moment by this news. She wondered what kind of strange place this was she had stumbled into. She stood by while the large dragon began tending to the baby. At the last moment, she realized that he was preparing to leave and take the baby with him.

"Wait!" she burst out. The dragon snapped his head around suspiciously. "I mean, *please* wait, Mister Dragon, sir." He snorted at that. "I think we got off to a bad start," Darien insisted. "I really was only trying to help your little sister. I thought she was hurt. I'm not from around here—I don't even know where *here* is—and I don't know anything about the people who took your mother."

She eased her way over to the baby and sat beside her. The little dragon promptly hummed and laid her head on Darien's lap. "Does she have a name yet? Mine's Darien."

The large dragon sighed impatiently. "Yes, her

name is Tabo. I am called Amani. Now, if there is nothing more, I need to get her somewhere safe so I can figure out how to get our parents back."

"Please wait," Darien pleaded. "Tell me more about what happened to your parents. Maybe there is something I can do to help."

"Help? Humans are not usually in the mood to help dragons. These days, humans are usually tricking and capturing and torturing and killing dragons. So what does one puny girl think *she* can do to help?"

Darien's face fell with disappointment. "I guess I don't know. I thought maybe . . . maybe I could help you think of a plan, if I knew more about what happened." She began to sniffle. "Look, I don't know what's going on, but I don't want to be left all alone. I'm lost. You're the only friends I have here." Her tears fell and left dark splatters on the ground. She rubbed the wetness off of her cheeks with an embarrassed swipe of her arm.

The dragon Amani mused over this while Darien waited nervously in silence. Finally he spoke to Tabo. "So she thinks we're friends, huh? Too soon to tell, I say. Still, I suppose we owe her something for helping you while I was gone." Amani's eyes softened. "I didn't know if you'd still be alive when I got back, little one. After Father was captured, I came back as fast as I could. I promise, I'll figure out a way to get them back.

I promise. . . ." Tabo looked deep into his eyes, then he gently rubbed his nose under her chin.

Amani turned once again to Darien. "Well, what should I do with you? I suppose I can take you home with us temporarily. I'm not sure you will fit in with the humans here, but I guess we can figure that out later. In any case, our family owes you a debt of gratitude, and I will not dishonor them by leaving you here."

Darien felt relieved. She wasn't sure if it was a good idea to leave the spot where she had first entered the forest. And there was no way to know if going back there would somehow lead her home. But if not, would she want to be stuck in this strange place alone—at night? If there were dragons here, what other creatures might be lurking about? No, Darien thought that it would be best to go with the dragons. At least Amani seemed to feel he owed her some help after what she did for Tabo, and she felt reasonably sure that he would protect her from any dangers they might encounter in the forest.

Darien forced her damp feet back into her shoes, while Amani leaned low to the ground to let Tabo climb onto his back. The little dragon instinctively crawled up to a spot between his shoulder blades, got a good grip with her front claws, and flattened herself against his body. Darien watched with fascination and then realized that she would have to find a place too.

"Um, where should I sit?" she asked.

"You can ride in front of Tabo, close to my neck. She'll help keep you from falling off, since you humans are built with such inferior claws. And by the way, dragons are not accustomed to being ridden by humans like ordinary pack horses, so don't get used to it."

Darien had once thought it would be exciting to ride a dragon, but now that she was faced with one, a not-especially-friendly one at that, the prospect seemed rather intimidating. Having no other choice, however, she swung her leg carefully over Amani's lowered neck and tried to get a good grip while avoiding the bony ridge that protected the back of the dragon's head.

"Are you ready, Human—er . . . Darien?" Amani rumbled.

"I guess so," she replied. The dragon crouched low for a second, and then, with a mighty leap, their bodies rose into the air. At the perfect moment, Amani's great wings unfurled from his back and strained to lift them higher and higher. "Hold on . . . you two," Amani puffed. "It's going . . . to be . . . a bumpy ride."

Darien held her breath as the ground lurched farther and farther away with each pump of Amani's wings. Every jolt threatened to topple Darien straight into the lake or, worse, into the thick forest. *What have I gotten myself into? I'll never be able to hold on for long this way.* She squeezed her eyes shut and clung tensely to

Amani's heaving back.

At last, with one final grunt of effort, the dragon lifted them, and suddenly all the jarring and jolting was gone. Amani stretched his wings to their widest, and they soared through the crisp air. When Darien was able to open her eyes again, she saw the tops of the trees far below. She was amazed at how fast the lake retreated behind them. At first, their flight followed a stream that fed into the lake. But Amani kept them on their own course, and gradually even the stream had faded from sight. Darien realized that it would do no good to try to keep track of their progress; she would simply have to trust that if she had to get back to the lake to return home, Amani would bring her back.

The air grew warmer after leaving the lake behind, and soon Darien's wet clothes began to dry, aided by the rushing wind. The lake had washed away the traces of dirt she had gotten on her clothes as a result of her race through the forest, but it had done nothing for the small tears, and it had also left behind a bit of a strange, stale smell. *I'm going to be in trouble if I ever get home from here*, she thought, noticing her torn hem and snagged tights. *There's no way I'll be able to explain this to my parents.*

As Darien grew accustomed to the steady, rhythmic rise and fall of the dragon's wings, her fears subsided and she began to enjoy the ride. She watched as the forest below gave way to a grassy plain. She glanced backward and was amused to note that Tabo had fallen asleep, her head snuggled against Darien's back.

Amani cleared his throat. "Ahem. Sorry for the bumpy start back there. I've always been considered pretty strong, especially since I'm not yet a full-grown dragon, but I guess I'm not used to carrying so much extra weight."

"Oh no, this is wonderful," Darien reassured him. "Really wonderful. It's better than I ever imagined." That was the truth. And even though Amani claimed he would be embarrassed to carry a human, Darien could see that he was pleased by her compliment.

"Are things so different in your land? There are friendships between humans and dragons?" Amani asked. It seemed as though he hadn't wanted to ask her anything, but curiosity had gotten the better of him.

"No," Darien replied. "There aren't *any* dragons where I come from. Not real ones, anyway. Only in stories and pictures. They're what we call make-believe or imaginary."

"Oh," Amani said, pondering for a moment.

Sensing an opening, Darien asked, "Amani? Can I ask where we're going? Is it far?"

"For a human on foot, far. For a dragon in flight, not so very far, but far enough out of the way to be frustrating. You see, if I were alone, I would have headed

43

straight to where I think they are taking Mother and Father. But because I have Tabo to take care of now, I have to get her to safety first." He politely didn't mention that Darien was slowing him down too. "So we're going to our caves in the hills, where Father's sister and her daughter are awaiting our return. It will be safe to leave Tabo there while I rescue my parents— if I can figure out how to do that, exactly." There was a pause as Amani considered the dilemma facing him. Darien was hesitant to push him for more information, yet she felt sure there was some way she could help, if only she could understand what was happening.

"Where are they taking your parents? You sound like you already know where they are going. And why do the people want them, anyway? I don't understand any of this. Why would anyone want to hurt such beautiful creatures?"

Amani seemed touched by her concern. He looked back at her almost kindly. "Thank you for saying that. Truly, you are not the same kind of human as I am used to. For the answer to your question is simple enough: greed. Dragons are hunted, captured, tortured, killed— solely to fulfill the pleasure and greed of these humans. Even the youngest human child here knows that when dragon scales are heated to the proper temperature, they turn into pure gold."

4

The Dragons' Tale

Darien was amazed by this extraordinary revelation. She looked down curiously at the smooth brown dragon scales underneath her hands. "And that's why they captured your parents: to take their scales and turn them into gold."

Amani nodded in response. "As strange as it seems to me, there was a time when our kind were protected, and dragons were happy to share our wealth—our scales—when they were shed naturally or after death. The strongest among us would breathe fire on them and melt them into gold, which could then be traded or given away as we chose. My father told me that in his youth dragons were quite generous, especially

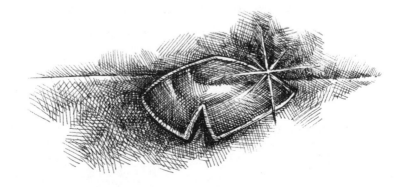

because they didn't really need anything. The king's laws protected the dragons, while the dragons protected him and the kingdom in return. Of course, ever since the king was murdered and the dragons were betrayed, we have become rather stingy."

"The king was *murdered*?" Darien broke in.

"Oh, that's a story better left for another time, and um,"—Amani glanced back at Darien nervously—"you might want to forget that I mentioned the part about murder. The official story is that he died from a problem with his heart, and although you'd never get my father to believe it, it might be best for you not to know any different."

Darien was intrigued by what had happened in this world. She desperately wanted to press Amani for more details, yet she knew she had to trust his judgment, so she forced herself to keep her questions to herself. For now, anyway.

"Where was I?" Amani asked.

"The dragons were betrayed, and you don't want to share with the humans anymore, right?"

"Ah yes. Well, of course hard feelings persisted on both sides. The more guarded the dragons became with their gold, the more greedy the humans became, and the more guarded the dragons became . . . and so on. The new king lifted the ban on harming dragons, and the hunting began. Since then, things have steadily fallen apart. Dragons were not very numerous to begin with. And having so many of our females taken during hatching is a terrible blow, especially since many of the new hatchlings can't survive without their mothers. If you hadn't been there to help Tabo, well . . . I don't want to think of it."

Darien blushed. "I just did the only thing I could think of. Anyway, she's fine now. That's all that matters. But why don't you all rise up against the humans until they agree to stop hunting your people? You seem so strong, and I bet you're awful fierce when you want to be."

Amani considered this for a moment. "I guess it's not that simple. You're right, dragons can be quite fierce when defending themselves or their families, but we're not generally what you'd call warlike creatures. We wouldn't have a clue how to organize ourselves for something like that. Plus, let's just say that dragons are *independent,* so working together is sometimes troublesome. Also, you speak as though we dragons are one united group, but that, too, has changed. A great rift has divided our race, and those of us on the wrong side have become outcasts, scattered about the countryside in small family groups or even alone."

"What happened?" Darien asked.

"You see, in the past, dragons only bonded with— married—other dragons of the same color. It wasn't a law, just a tradition. Then one day, our good king Dex was casually talking with a small group of advisers and friends, and they wondered among themselves why it was that dragons only partnered with others of similar color. They wondered whether any dragons ever felt trapped by having to choose a mate this way, or if some would have been happier choosing a mate of a different color. They went on to guess at the reasons why dragons behaved this way, and eventually their discussion turned in other directions. But the seed had been planted in the mind of a young dragon in the king's guard. It so happened that Audric, my father, was on duty that day in the garden. Although he wasn't interested in bonding with anyone yet, the seed grew as he thought about it and talked about it with his friends.

"Word of this radical idea spread through the young dragons, and of course the elders heard of it too, though they were not interested in discussing it. There was nothing to talk about, really, since there is no actual reason why the dragons had done things the way they had; it was simply a tradition. Perhaps long ago there was more to it, but if so, the meaning has been lost to us.

"Well, in short, my father was not the first to mate outside his color, but the idea had grown and grown in him, and it came to full bloom two years later when he first laid eyes on Brisa, my mother. Quite a few of the younger dragons had chosen to mix-mate by then. Though the elders certainly didn't approve, it seemed like we would remain at peace, especially after my father did it—he was in the guard and held high in the king's personal favor. Given time, we might have learned to accept one another again. But things happened fast after King Dex was . . . gone . . . and it became shamefully easy for the new king to convince the elders and pure-mates to turn against the mixed-mates.

"For dragons, the worst finally happened when the first hatchlings came into their colors. Instead of being a solid color like one parent or the other, they came out as a mixture of both. You can't judge it by how I look; my colors are plain compared to some of the more outlandish combinations I've seen."

Darien noticed that Amani was mostly brown with some red counter-shading on his underbelly, and the translucent skin forming his wings was a similar dark red. Otherwise he was fairly plain, though Darien thought his particular shade of brown was rather lovely, reminding her of stark trees in wintertime and the rich fudge her grandmother used to make at Christmas.

"I think you look cool," Darien commented.

Amani huffed. "Well, the pure-mates were horrified, even the ones who were closely related to the hatchlings. The elders told the mixed-mates either to rid themselves of their freak babies and part from their chosen partner or to leave the dragon homeland.

"It sickens me to say that there were a few who chose to stay, but my parents and many others appealed to the king—the new king, Nevin Radburn, not King Dex—to grant them a land of their own. He consented, but when the dragons gathered together to leave for the new land, it turned out to be a trick. The king figured that no one would care about these exiles, and he and his minions would be free to kill them off and keep the gold for themselves. But they underestimated the dragons' fury at being betrayed. The men were no match for the dragons and were forced to flee back to the royal city. Yet the dragons weren't through. They flew into a rage and attacked the city they had spent a lifetime defending. The people had no choice except to run, and the dragons were not idle after the humans left. They carried off what they could of the food and then destroyed everything else, leaving nothing for the people to return to except stone rubble. They say you can barely even tell where the great castle stood." Amani's voice lowered wistfully. "I wish I could have seen it just once. Father told me it was magnificent in King Dex's time."

Darien felt saddened by the tale of the dragons' lost homeland, the ruined city, and the innocent humans forced to leave with the bad ones. "So what happened to the dragons? And where did the people go?"

"For the dragons, there is not much to tell. Some of the related families tried to stick together, like we do with my aunt's family; the rest went out on their own. Remember the hatchlings? The parents were desperate to find safety and shelter for the young ones. So they scattered, living in obscurity and hoping to one day hear news of dragons gathering and thriving in a new land. My father had recently begun talking with a group of traveling dragons, trying to convince them to settle near us. But then Father's sister's mate was killed, and the travelers were scared away.

"As for the humans, you should know that the royal city was not their only place to live. There are other settlements, though none as grand or as isolated from other races. The king decided to make himself a new royal city in Garddington, under Mount Garddrock. Many people already living in Garddington resented this, but they were not going to openly refuse their king. There was a rumor, however, that a faction still loyal to King Dex fled and has not been heard from again."

"And this Mount Garddrock—" Darien asked, "is that where they're taking your parents?"

"Yes, I believe so. I've never been there, but I've seen it from a distance and heard about it from my father. The city lies within old underground mines, so as you can imagine, it would be impossible for me to free my parents secretly. There's not much room to fly, and I'm sure they would notice a dragon stomping his way through their tunnels. No, I think my only chance is to gather as many dragons as I can find on my way and hope they will agree to help me. If there are enough of us and we are strong enough, I have to believe we can force the humans to free my parents."

Amani paused. "It's odd though," he mused.

"What?"

"That they were captured instead of killed outright like all the others. Of course, that's good, but I wonder why the hunters would go through all the extra trouble. It was no small feat for them to take two dragons alive and haul them all the way back to the city."

Amani became silent as he and Darien contemplated the gravity of their situation. While she thought about the impossible-sounding task ahead of Amani, Darien noticed that the landscape had changed yet again. Below, rippling green plains had long since given way to smoothly rounded hills, which were becoming increasingly rocky-looking the farther they flew. Appearing out of the mist ahead of them was a chain of imposing mountains that reached as far as they could see on either side.

Amani's head began to sway from left to right

until finally he exclaimed, "Ah! Here it is," and they began to descend from the air. His wings tucked in, and they dove toward a clearing in the sparse forest of the hillside. Darien gripped the dragon tightly, anticipating a rough landing, but in a blur his large wings opened to their fullest—mere moments before they would have crashed onto the rocky ground—and they touched down without even a bounce.

Tabo scrambled easily off Amani's back, already stable on her feet, though unable to do much with her wings yet. Darien followed and tried unsteadily to walk, though it felt as if the ground was rising and falling under her feet. Amani took a moment to catch his breath, then cautioned Darien to stand far behind his back.

"We need to be prepared for a hostile welcome. I don't think my aunt will be happy that I've brought a human to our home." With that said, Amani stood next to Tabo and let out a strange, piercing whistle.

Moments passed. Darien's eyes darted from side to side, trying to anticipate where the aunt would emerge from the trees. Finally they heard two short whistles in response. Amani repeated the two whistles back, and another moment later a large dragon crept out with her back hunched over and her nostrils flaring.

"Aunt Gallia," Amani called, "it's safe to come out. Come meet my new baby sister."

A dull brown dragon with sad eyes approached Tabo and they rubbed noses. "Oh, you are beautiful," she whispered.

"Her name is Tabo," Amani added.

Aunt Gallia abruptly pulled up to her full height, and Darien saw a large scar across her chest. The dragon had spotted Darien and was becoming extremely agitated.

"Human! Human!" she screamed.

Amani stepped in her way and prevented her from lunging at Darien.

"Where are your parents, Amani?" Aunt Gallia demanded. "You signaled it was safe! Why is there a human here?"

Amani had to raise his voice considerably to be heard. "Aunt Gallia, calm down! She's just a young girl. I'll explain," he said, still keeping himself between Darien and his enraged aunt. "We need to talk, but I don't have much time." Amani led Aunt Gallia aside, and he told her briefly of his parents' capture and how Darien had come to save Tabo's life.

Meanwhile, Darien made her way on quivering legs to where Tabo was laying. She marveled at the way Tabo's skin was hardening and cracking into small shapes that were even now starting to resemble scales. It was amazing how fast the little dragon was beginning to look like a miniature of her brother, although

Tabo had more of a russet color
to her shimmery scales rather
than brown. Also, she appeared
to have dark markings around
her eyes that turned up at the
outer corners, and similarly dark
swashes on her sides, giving her a much more exotic
look than either Amani or Aunt Gallia.

Darien found herself again with Tabo's head in
her lap. The little one seemed to like the way she
scratched the sensitive spot in front of her ears where
her horns would one day grow. Darien also noticed
that occasionally little nickel-size round bugs would fly
over and land on Tabo's back, biting and irritating her
skin. They seemed harmless to Darien, so she carefully
flicked them away with a short stick whenever she saw
them.

From across the clearing, Aunt Gallia kept a wary
eye on Darien. As she listened to Amani's story and
saw how caring and affectionate Darien seemed to be
with Tabo, her eyes gradually softened. Amani finished
relating what had happened, and they headed over to
where Darien and Tabo sat. Darien removed Tabo's
head from her lap and jumped to her feet in front
of the towering female, hoping to avoid arousing any
further anger from the dragon. Aunt Gallia lowered
her head and scrutinized Darien briefly.

"It seems as though I owe you an apology, child," she said in her wavering voice. "I'm sorry for giving little Tabo's friend and rescuer such a rude welcome."

"Oh, um, that's okay, ma'am," Darien stammered. "Amani told me what happened—I understand why you would be angry. I hope you know that I would never want to hurt any dragon." She paused, then laughed. "Not like I could anyway. I'm just a kid, you know."

Amani snorted softly at this, amused, but Aunt Gallia looked very seriously into Darien's eyes. "I wouldn't be too sure about that. Sometimes the smallest creature can make the biggest impact. Look at those fire-fleas," she said, eyeing the bugs near Tabo's back. "They're small and usually quite harmless. But if a mature one stings just right, underneath the scales, it can actually paralyze a full-grown dragon for a whole day. So don't underestimate yourself."

Amani gave Darien a thoughtful look, then cleared his throat. "Ahem. . . . Aunt, time is growing short if I hope to reach Mount Garddrock tonight. I assumed I could leave Tabo with you, but we'll have to figure out what to do with Darien. I wondered if the elves might agree to take her into their care, but neither of us can take her to find them right now—if they're even still around." Amani began to pace nervously through the clearing.

"Did you say elves?" Darien asked, barely containing

her excitement.

"Shush, girl," Amani cut her off. "There's no time now. I must leave as soon as possible."

"Not before you get something to eat," Aunt Gallia insisted. "You have no idea when you'll have another chance, and you'll need your energy." (Inside, Darien cringed to think what in the world a dragon would eat.) "I know you're in a hurry, but at least go to the KuaKua trees and get some nuts." Amani seemed to consider arguing, saw his aunt's stern face, then grunted and turned away.

Aunt Gallia watched him disappear through the trees. Then she turned to Darien. "And what about you, child? We should find you some food too, yes?"

Darien began to answer, "No, ma'am. I'm all right." But her stomach betrayed her by gurgling loudly. "Well, maybe I could have something. Is there anything around here that I can eat?" She began to think about how the characters in all her books always managed to find fruits or berries to eat just when they needed them; or even better, they would be fed magical foods by kind elves or fairies. Unfortunately, Darien had only her non-magical dragon friends, and all the surrounding vegetation suddenly seemed unfamiliar and suspicious.

Aunt Gallia saw Darien look skeptically around the clearing. "I'm sure we can find something for you. To start with, there is fresh water from a spring inside our cave. What else? . . . Oh, these leaves over here," she said, pointing to some weedy-looking plants sprouting up from the ground. To Darien they looked a lot like dandelion leaves, but they didn't have either the cheery yellow flower or the puffy seed flower. She grabbed a handful of leaves and followed Aunt Gallia toward their cave home. Before they reached the opening, the large dragon bent over and smelled along the ground. "Hmm . . . over here. Yes. Would you eat mushrooms?" she asked.

Darien crinkled her nose slightly but replied, "I guess. Are they safe for me to eat? Where I come from, wild mushrooms can sometimes make you sick, I think."

"It's the same here," Aunt Gallia replied. "But I've seen humans eat this kind, so I'm sure you will be fine."

Darien busied herself by carefully picking through the small patch of fungi. Some of the mushrooms were clearly no good, but enough were smooth and firm and without blemishes so that she quickly had more than she could carry back to the dragons' cave.

Detour to the Volcano

After eating enough of the bitter greens and mushrooms to take the edge off her hunger and drinking deeply from the fresh-water spring, Darien left the cave while Aunt Gallia and her daughter, Mala, prepared to get Tabo settled down for another nap. She squinted as she emerged from the darkness into the tree-filtered sunlight and walked back to the middle of the clearing where Amani had just finished crunching up the last of his food, leaving large rust-colored shells around him on the ground. Darien turned a curious eye their way, but Amani warned her not to eat them or touch them, explaining that they were extremely spicy and hot. He swept them aside into a pile with a brisk swipe of his tail.

Darien walked with Amani toward the outer edge of the clearing. They were met by Aunt Gallia, who explained that Tabo had fallen asleep and Gallia's daughter, Mala, was watching over her.

Amani looked from Darien to Aunt Gallia and sighed deeply. "Well, it appears the time is upon me. I must go to find my parents and any who I can convince to join me along the way."

"Oh, Amani," Aunt Gallia said, slowly shaking her head. "Do you really think this is the best way? What are the chances you'll be able to find other dragons willing to help, especially when you have no time to spare seeking them out? I have a bad feeling about this."

A look of intense frustration screwed up Amani's face. "I don't know, Aunt! But there is no other choice, no other way I can see. Trust me, the thought of leaving Tabo with no direct family left is tearing me apart."

"You know that if anything happened to you, I would take care of Tabo like my own daughter," Aunt Gallia reassured softly.

"Thank you, Aunt," Amani replied. "But you know what I'm saying. It's not the same."

Aunt Gallia nodded. Amani looked at her with a mixture of sadness and gratefulness, then readied himself to spring into the air.

"Wait!" Darien said. Amani stopped in mid-crouch and looked at her impatiently. "I might have an idea. You need more dragons to go with you, right? Okay, so what if we go to the pure dragons and ask them to help you? You said they stayed behind at the dragon homeland, so you must know where they are, and there must be at least some who would join you. Then you wouldn't have to spend a bunch of time trying to find the other exiles scattered all over the place."

"I wish it were that simple," Amani told her gently, noticing the look of hope on Darien's face. "But I'm afraid that wouldn't work. I'd have to go through the high elder Grisha, and there is little chance he would agree to meet with me, much less listen and help me."

"But you said your father was so well respected and in the king's guard."

"And so his was an even worse act of betrayal to the elders," Amani replied. "As my father's son, I would not be listened to or even admitted into Grisha's presence. Now I really must go."

"*I* will go," Darien firmly stated.

"Now, wait just a minute—"

"I will go," Darien said again. "What's happening here is wrong, no matter what colors you are, no matter what kind of thing you are. I am only a human child, as you've pointed out, but even I can see that this is not right. So if there's a chance that this old dragon will let me talk to him, you have to take me with you. You have to give me a chance to convince him to send help with you. If there's anything I've learned from all the books I've read it's that you can't let the bullies win;

you have to stand up to them or they keep doing bad stuff until everyone is afraid of them. Please, Amani, please let me try. If there's even a tiny chance he'll listen to me . . ."

Amani shook his head and frowned at Aunt Gallia. "No, no I don't like this at all."

Aunt Gallia looked intently at Darien for a moment, then back at Amani. "It is against all hope that you can succeed alone, Amani," she said. "Let the girl try. If even one dragon joins you, maybe you'll have a chance. It won't even take you very far out of your way." She paused and shrugged, "If nothing else, perhaps they will at least have information about the humans that will help you. Either way, you must decide now and be on your way, even though I hate your leaving on this terrible quest."

Amani stood silently and closed his eyes for a tense minute. When he finally looked down at Darien, she returned his gaze anxiously.

"Let it be," he said, "that the human child will take on the great elder Grisha himself, all luck to her. Climb on my back once again, and we will do what we must do, as much as I hate to waste any time with those thick-skulled stubborn fools."

* * *

Gray majestic peaks flowed past on Darien's left side as she and Amani sliced through the air. With the weight of Tabo gone, Amani had whisked Darien away and was now swiftly approaching the most unusual part of the mountain range. Standing boldly between two lesser cliffs was the largest mountain. It had no peak, just a steep crater at the top. It was covered in lush vegetation, yet Darien could see that the ground underneath was of the deepest black.

"It looks like a volcano!" she said with surprise.

"Yes, you're partly right," Amani answered. "It used to be a volcano long before the humans lived here. That is why it makes the perfect home for dragons: there is a fire that, even now, heats the earth far below the surface, keeping the home caves comfortably close to our natural body temperature. I have no memory of living there, so this cold doesn't bother me much." (Darien noticed she was warm even though the wind was rushing past her.) "But my father says his bones ache nearly all the time, now that he doesn't have the heat to rejuvenate him."

"So . . . is that where we're going?" Darien asked with trepidation.

Amani noticed her anxiety and reassured her. "Yes, but I don't think the main meeting chambers are as hot since they're up higher, and you won't be terribly uncomfortable. Also, there is a good chance

that we won't be admitted into the caves at all, and we'll be forced to continue our rescue alone. Try not to be too disappointed; we'll figure something out either way. . . . We have to," he added quietly.

Darien closed her eyes and tried to calm herself, but nervousness was sinking in. She forced herself to breathe deeply and focus on the anger she felt when she thought about Tabo not having parents to love her and protect her. She wanted to be strong and convincing when she confronted the elder dragons, though Darien feared she would only appear pleading and desperate.

Amani seemed to spot the place he had been searching for and took a steep dive directly toward the mountainside. Before they reached the cave opening, he turned his head briefly. "Don't worry, just do your best and be quick so we can get on our way," he told her.

Now Darien felt hotter inside, burning with a determination to prove Amani wrong. She pressed her body flat against his back as they approached the cave. With a casual snap of his wings, Amani ducked into a large opening and landed without a sound. Darien dismounted with more confidence this time, although it still took a few moments to get her land-legs back.

"Do you know where this cave leads?" Darien whispered.

"Yes, I have a pretty good idea we're in the right place, if my father's description of it was correct," he answered. "And there's no need to whisper. We have nothing to hide. Besides, they already know we're here."

Darien squinted into the dim depths of the tunnel and barely saw two large yellowish eyes peering back. A dusty-gray dragon approached and eyed the two newcomers with a bold glare. He glanced at Darien, then turned his attention toward Amani.

"I never thought I'd see the day when a dragon would turn into a mule, even one so . . . *colorful* as yourself," he said haughtily. "I mean, really, carrying a human around like baggage? It's just not dignified. Or was the little thing riding you like a pet?"

The normally proud and quick-tempered Amani managed to ignore this mockery, since getting into an argument at this point would waste precious time. Instead, he replied, "When you're all done insulting us, we have urgent business to attend to. We must speak with the Elder Council at once."

"Really?" the gray asked, condescension thick in his voice. "And what makes you think they will agree to see the likes of you? Go away, they're much too busy to deal with a pathetic eyesore of a dragon and whatever this scrap of bones is that you've dragged in with you." He turned to saunter away, but it was Darien's temper that flared at him.

"Hey!" she shouted. "We came a long way to see your old council, and we're not leaving until they hear what we have to say. Now, please tell them that Darien of the Blue Lake and Amani, son of—" Darien looked at Amani for help.

"Audric," Amani said.

"Son of Audric," she continued, "are here, and we respectfully insist on meeting with them." Darien stood alongside Amani with her tightly fisted hands on her hips, but the gray dragon taunted her with his laughter. However, he did retreat deeper into the tunnel, speaking to himself intentionally loud enough for both Amani and Darien to hear.

"It seems the little one has more fire than the

big one. I wonder if she'll be as bold in the council chamber. We shall see, eh? We shall see. . . ."

When the gray was out of sight, Amani rolled his eyes toward the ceiling of the cave. "So you're Darien of the Blue Lake now?" he teased.

"Well, it sounds better than Darien of Cherry Blossom Drive." Amani didn't respond. After a minute, Darien asked, "What do you think he meant about the council chamber? Should I be worried?"

"I don't know anything about the chamber except that it's where the elders meet. He probably just meant for you to feel nervous and intimidated."

"It's working," Darien admitted.

"We can leave anytime, you know. You don't have to do this," Amani said.

"I do," said Darien emphatically. "We're here already, so it would be stupid to just leave. Anyway, it was my idea to come, and I mean to follow through with it." Darien spoke firmly, yet her hands felt shaky and her stomach was queasy. *I wish they'd hurry up so I can get this over with*, she thought.

They waited in silence except for the impatient scratching of Amani's claws against the rocky floor. Just when Darien was about to snap at Amani to quit making his annoying sounds and when Amani was on the verge of telling Darien they couldn't afford to waste any more time, they heard the steady thump of heavy footsteps approaching. The gray came without stealth this time and lazily returned to the two anxious friends.

"So, the full council is absolutely not going to bother gathering for you; I could've told you that before," the gray scoffed. "I spoke with Grisha himself, and he refuses to speak with you, son of . . . Whomever." Amani moved as if to leave without another word for this fool's errand, but the gray continued. "But he is curious about this small human. He ordered you to attend him in the chamber at once, or else go and leave him to his rest."

Darien flashed a hopeful smile at Amani, and they started to follow the gray until he pointed toward Amani.

"No!" he exclaimed. "You won't be stepping one multicolored toe into the council chamber. Only the girl is permitted into Grisha's presence."

With wide eyes, Darien looked to Amani for direction. "It's up to you," he shrugged. "I will wait if you still want to go. But please remember our urgency."

The Chamber and
the Charlots

Few humans in recent history had ever seen the great council chamber of the dragons. Technically speaking, Darien wasn't seeing it either; it was so dark she couldn't make out any sort of detail. After a long, uncomfortable walk through the dim tunnel, with a tentative hold on the gray dragon's foreleg for guidance, Darien was left to experience the chamber alone. The darkness seemed oppressive, made worse by the stifling heat. The air was very stuffy, even though it moved across Darien's skin in waves of alternating warm and hot. No sound originated from the cave, but she could almost feel echoes in the wind and in her bones. *I'd be shivering for sure right now if it weren't so hot! Amani's smart, but I'm not trusting his judgment about temperature ever again,* she thought. It was impossible for Darien to gauge just how long she waited; in reality, it was only about five minutes, yet the lack of light and companionship made the time stretch ever so much longer.

Abruptly, in spite of the heat, goose bumps prickled up on Darien's arms, and she knew she was no longer alone in the chamber. Some distance away and about fifteen feet up, two garnet-red eyes smoldered. The dragon belonging to them approached while Darien stood anxiously, straining to see in the dark. With an unexpected roar, an enormous flame burst from the dragon's jaws! Darien screamed and ducked down, covering her head with her hands, but the fire was not directed at her. It leaped from the dragon's mouth toward the side of the cave where the swirling wind grabbed the flame and ignited torches along the wall, surrounding Darien in a wide circle of harsh light. Several loud echoing booms sounded in the distance and a moment later the winds died down. Darien, stunned, stayed in a low crouch and looked up at the dragon with fearful eyes, while he looked down on her from the ledge in front of his cave.

Even with her limited experience with dragons, Darien sensed this one was older than old. He had probably once been very large and impressive, but now he was stooped and bent. His dark green skin sagged off of his bones and he was covered in deep wrinkles. His eyes, however, were still stern and calculating, and one would have been very foolish indeed to mistake his aged looks for weakness.

Darien stood, still looking up at the elder dragon, even though the fear and heat were making her a little dizzy. Gathering her courage, Darien met the dragon's eyes and addressed him in a voice that wavered just the smallest bit.

"Th-Thank you for meeting with me, sir," she said, hoping she wasn't breaking dragon etiquette by speaking first. She hesitated, waiting to hear if the dragon would answer, then continued when he remained silent. "I'm here because we really need your help. You see, my friend's parents were captured by some bad people and taken to their mountain—I'm afraid they're going to be killed, for their gold, you know—and it's going to be nearly impossible to rescue them all by ourselves. I'm sure an important dragon like you could convince others to come with us and help—"

"Who are you?" Grisha's rasping voice demanded. "You talk strangely and dress strangely; you even smell strange. Clearly you're not from here. Just who do you think you are to come here, wasting my time, asking for favors for your filthy mongrel friend? Oh yes, I know who it is that waits, dirtying my doorstep. The name of Audric is still well known to us; we take much care in remembering those who turned their back on our noble ways. So the traitor's son avoids us and sends a little girl instead to beg us for help, eh? I think Audric would be ashamed to see such weakness."

Though Grisha's voice was dry and gruff, it dripped with scorn as he gazed in his arrogance down at Darien. She didn't know whether it was the heated air or her anger that was making her face so fiery hot, and Darien struggled hard to keep her temper under control. She knew that lashing out at this crusty old dragon would be the worst mistake, no matter how much she wanted to defend Amani's honor.

"Well?" Grisha barked. "Explain now or get out! I want to know who you are and where you came from." His eyes narrowed with suspicion while he waited for Darien's answer.

Darien took as deep of a breath as she could in the thick air and tried to answer calmly, hoping to find words that would appease Grisha. She admitted that he was right, she did indeed come from another place. How she came to be in their land was harder to explain, since she didn't understand it herself. Darien did her best to describe all that had happened, but Grisha seemed very reluctant to trust what she was saying; he attacked her with endless questions, trying to catch her off guard, as if hoping one time her answers would change and she would accidentally reveal some other secret reason for being there.

"Look," Darien said with exasperation, "it doesn't matter how I got here—we can keep going over and over it, even though I really can't explain it any more than

I already have—but the fact remains that two dragons, dragons *just like you*, will probably die if you don't send help with us."

Grisha nearly spat his reply out through his clenched jaws: "Those creatures are no longer fit to be called dragons, and they are not like me at all. I stayed true to our honorable traditions. I am not the one who turned my back on my duties and community. I am not the one who broke our society apart for my selfish gains. It was I, Grisha, who held the faithful ones together and forced them to stay with our ancient ways."

"How can you be so stubborn that you can't see it's not worth the lives of your fellow dragons? Can't you see how stupid it is to fight about what colors you are on the outside? You're all the same on the inside," Darien said, her anger and impatience beginning to show.

"What did you call me?" Grisha said in a terrifyingly soft whisper.

"I—I didn't mean that *you* were s-stupid," Darien said, backtracking, "I only meant that how you were acting . . ." Her heart began to throb violently in her chest, fearing what Grisha would do if he became enraged with her.

The aged dragon leaped from his elevated cave with an agility none would have guessed he still had.

In three great paces, he stood towering over Darien, the light from the torches dancing devilishly over his sunken features. His fierce eyes blazed as Darien tried to stand her ground, then he uttered a hard, cruel, cold, and humorless laugh.

"Ha! I shouldn't have been worried that you had some hidden motivation for being here, that your story was a clever ruse to trick us into revealing our treasures or secrets. You are only what you say you are: a girl from nowhere, ignorant of our proud and tragic history, on a foolhardy quest. Give up now. You will not survive your mission, and if the traitors die as well, I will not be sorry. Now, get out, before I decide to end your journey right here and now."

"But I don't know the way—"

"Go!"

* * *

Darien never knew how she made it back through the tunnel alone and nearly blind in the darkness. She only remembered stumbling along, her hand scraping painfully against the wall for guidance. Her ears rang from the deafening roar of Grisha's bellowing voice. She felt the suffocating humidity and heat lessen gradually as she left the area of the council chamber.

After what seemed an eternity, Amani's pacing silhouette appeared. In an instant, he read defeat in Darien's expression and prepared to fly. Darien flung her small body onto Amani's back, and without a word they leaped into the air.

With every breath, Darien sobbed, overwhelmed by her failure and with the reality of her new situation finally sinking in. *What was I thinking?* she berated herself. *We wasted so much time! How could I have been so stupid to think I could make a difference in all this? I don't have any idea what I'm up against with these dragon kidnappers. . . .I don't have a clue how I'm going to get Amani's parents back, if they're even still alive. . . . and now I have nowhere else to go. . . .*

Darien's crying slowly subsided. She took a deep breath and let out a long trembling sigh. Then she remained quiet for a while, letting the feel of the wind and the steady beat of Amani's wings calm her. *Well, I volunteered for this job, didn't I? There's nothing else to do but to keep my word. I promised to help, and I guess I can only do my best. I hope something will come to me when we get to the city. I know one thing: I am not depending on anyone else's help—I have to assume that I will be completely on my own there.* As Darien resigned herself to the job ahead, she laid her cheek against Amani's smooth scales and felt comforted by the warmth emanating from them.

Through Darien's inner struggle, Amani remained patient and silent. When she had calmed down sufficiently, he said, "I can't deny that I am very frustrated that none of the pure dragons were willing to join us and that we haven't found any other help. It was not unexpected, but frustrating nevertheless. Yet I have to say how much it means to me that you would even try to confront the elders on behalf of my family. You were very brave—many dragons would never have dared to do as much—but I will understand if you want me to continue on my own. When you agreed to help, you may not have understood what we are up against and how dangerous it might be. Perhaps now you have a better idea of how serious things are and want to change your mind."

After a few moments thinking about Amani's words, Darien raised her head up and let the cooling wind tug at the unruly strands of her blowing hair. She felt the last of her tears disappear from her cheeks.

"We have to do this, no matter what it takes," she said, her voice firm.

"It's truly all right if you want to stop," Amani insisted. "I appreciate that you wanted to try to help, but you don't owe me anything—on the contrary, I owe it to you to keep you safe and not drag you into unknown dangers ahead."

"I am not quitting now," Darien said. "But we need a plan or something, since it looks like we're going to have to do this all by ourselves."

"Yes," Amani agreed, "but first things first. What happened with Grisha? I don't want to upset you, but can you tell me about it?" Darien's hands clenched tighter against his back when he mentioned the elder dragon.

"Oh, he made me so frustrated! He kept grilling me over and over: Who was I? Where did I come from? What did I really want? To explain how I got here again. He was suspicious and he was grouchy, and he was really, really mean at the end, calling your parents traitors and saying he wouldn't care if they didn't survive. I know he was going out of his way to seem scary to me, too. Amani, I tried so hard to be polite and keep myself from getting mad at him, but he wouldn't even listen."

Darien was quiet for a few moments until Amani glanced back to see her deep in thought.

"You know," she said finally, "I realize that I don't understand everything that happened with you dragons in the past and that I'm an outsider here, but I just don't get how the fight could still be so important after all this time, more important than helping other dragons in trouble. It just doesn't seem right to me."

"I certainly won't defend the elders' actions," Amani said. "I guess the only thing you need to understand is that the older generation is very stubborn and proud and very close-minded. They think they're doing the noble thing, and they want to uphold what they see as their sacred traditions. They are too blind to see that the traditions will die out either way. Change is bound to happen, sooner or later, for better or worse. If they would've only embraced the changes, perhaps. . . . Oh no, not now—"

Darien looked from side to side, straining her eyes to see. "What's wrong, Amani?"

"Look below," he answered bluntly, preoccupied with the unexpected danger.

"I don't see any— oh, wait a second," Darien squinted down. At first she didn't see anything except the scrubby trees far below, but then she saw what looked like a dark pulsating cloud moving closer to them. It was no ordinary cloud, however. It appeared to be following their attempts to avoid it. Amani pumped his wings hard and fast, raising them higher with each thrust. No matter how fast they flew, the cloud seemed to keep gaining on them until Darien could see that it wasn't a cloud at all but a flock of some kind of flying creatures. They had dark gray softball-size bodies and short, fragile-looking wings that flapped in such an awkward way it would've been funny, had they not been so clearly intent on attacking.

"Amani, what are those things?" Darien asked. "Are they dangerous?"

"They're called charlots; they're fire-eaters," he answered, panting heavily. "Won't hurt you. Not sure about me. Bad to have so many at once. Hold tight." Amani stopped talking, straining with the effort to outrun and outmaneuver the charlots.

Soon enough it became clear that they couldn't escape. Somehow, even though they were clumsy and small, the charlots were catching up. Darien began to hear the strange beating sound of the creatures' flopping wings, louder and closer with each passing moment. Every muscle in her body was tense as she gripped Amani's back. Darien fought against the tide of panic rising inside.

"Amani, what are we going to do?" she shrieked.

"Hold on!" Amani yelled back. "They'll go straight for me. But if you get the chance to kick any of them off, do it! They're not very tough, but they'll keep attacking until I blow fire to get them away."

"Can't you just do it now?"

"No! Dragon fire makes them crazy and causes them to give off a horrible gas too sickening to breathe. Literally, it's poisonous. Doesn't matter anyway, I can't make fire yet—at least not much—" Amani broke off as the first of the hideous creatures came within reach of the dragon's mighty jaws, which snapped shut just inches away from the small, bulging, hairy body of the charlot. It dropped away to avoid Amani's bite, but another one was already flying in to attack the other side. Before it could reach them, Amani's tail whipped around and smacked it with a solid pop. Over and over, Amani defended them from the flying assault, but there seemed to be no end to the swarm of charlots darting in and out.

Finally, one of the beasts was able to clamp a

mouthful of sharp teeth into the bony part of Amani's left wing. It didn't hurt much through the dragon's tough skin, but his flying became more unstable and erratic when he tried to shake the creature off. Darien's already cramped hands managed an even tighter grip as she kicked it off with a squeal of disgust. Before she could take a breath, two more attached themselves to Amani's opposite wing as the fierce dragon began to tire from the relentless assault. Still, his tail was a blur as it slashed the air, his body writhed from side to side, his head lashed out at every approaching attacker. Many of the charlots were knocked away, but so many more were diving and dodging their way in toward Amani's body.

Darien did her best to help, yet every moment it became harder to hold on. The charlots were ignoring the girl clinging to the dragon's back, their simple minds focused on their large prey. Two of them swerved to avoid Amani's biting teeth, collided with each other, and bounced straight at Darien's head. Instinctively, her hand flew up to slap them away from her face, and suddenly she felt weightless.

With a nauseating lurch, Darien dropped away from Amani's twisting back, both hands scrambling to grab on. Then she found herself falling toward the distant land below. The wind rushing past Darien's face rippled her skin and left her feeling breathless, unable to find a pocket of air to fill her lungs. She struggled not to pass out, which at least kept her too distracted to think that she was almost certainly falling to her doom.

Darien Makes a Difficult Decision

Darkness came and wrapped itself around the girl like a tight swaddling blanket. Neither the wind rustling gently through the trees nor the heavily pacing footsteps could make the darkness loosen its embrace. The girl wandered in the darkness and lost herself in its depths.

She begged the darkness to stay, but it began to pull away from her. She chased it down, willing it to continue, fear gripping her chest and right arm. *Please stay*, she pleaded. *I am afraid of what will be here if you go.*

* * *

A throbbing heat encircled Darien's upper right arm. She gasped and her eyes snapped open. Afternoon light stippled her body, winking through the canopy of leaves overhead. Jagged, broken branches and tattered leaves lined an open path to the clear sky above and to the left. She barely had time to wonder where she was and what had happened when Amani's concerned face filled her view.

"Amani," she cried, "what happened?"

"Before we get into that, how does your arm feel? Can you move it?" he asked.

Darien sat up slowly and examined her arm. There was a wide red ring past her elbow, but that didn't hurt nearly as much as her shoulder did. She could bend her elbow easily, but when she stretched and tried to make a wide circle with her arm, the pain became almost unbearable.

"It's not too bad," she said to Amani, although her strained expression told him it was worse than she was letting on. "C'mon, I want to know what happened."

"Well, there's not much to tell, but if you feel up to it, climb on my back and I will tell you as we travel," Amani said. He bent low so Darien could get on easily, and when they reached a big enough clearing in the trees they took flight once again.

Amani told Darien how he had realized immediately that she had fallen, so he had knocked the remaining charlots away with his wings and dove through the air to grab her with his large claws.

His brief description didn't do justice to how he had powerfully flown up in the air, then twisted

downward in a blurred corkscrew, batting
the charlots away with his wings. He
didn't tell her how he had shot straight as
an arrow toward her, his wings tucked to
his sides, his body cutting through the air
so quickly he could hardly see. He didn't
tell her how he had clasped her arm just
a moment before she reached the treetops
and they both had crashed through leaves
and branches until finally making it safely
to the ground. He didn't tell her how he
had sat and worried over her as she lay
unconscious on the patchy grass.

"I'm sorry about your arm," Amani
said. "Are you still in a lot of pain?"

"It's feeling much better already,"
Darien said. She laid her head against
Amani's warm back and wrapped her arms
as far as she could around the sides of his
neck in a tentative hug. "Thanks for saving
me, Amani," she whispered. He pretended
not to hear.

"Are you absolutely sure you want to
do this?" Amani asked as Darien tried to
gently stretch her sore arm. "It is not yet
too late to take you down to the forest,
but it soon will be. See how the ground

is becoming more rocky and barren? We are getting closer to the mines, and there will be no safe place for you to wait for me once we pass the edge of the tree line. I am disappointed that we haven't seen even one other dragon who might have come to help. That is going to make our job even more difficult. My plan to go in forcefully, with other dragons by my side, is obviously not going to happen. I would understand and encourage you to stay here, where you'll be much safer. I am not giving up without a fight, but just so we're clear, I might be fighting an impossible battle."

"That's all the more reason to stick together," Darien said. "You need all the help you can get. Besides, you are not leaving me alone to fight off more of those charlots or something even worse. I don't know what kind of strange things might be living down there."

Amani considered this for a moment, then agreed. "You're right, I probably need your help, more than I want to admit. Just so you know, if I had any other choice, I would not be dragging a child into this. How the elders and pure-mates would laugh to think of big, proud Amani needing help from a little human girl," he scoffed.

"You know what, Amani? They're the ones who should be laughed at, for being foolish and old and stuck in their ways. After a while, they will all die out, and no one is going to remember them for their bravery or loyalty, just that they hid themselves away thinking they were better than everyone else. They should be ashamed that a little girl will try to do what's right and they won't. You shouldn't even care what they might think— oh, look straight ahead, there," Darien broke off, seeing the end of the trees a short distance in front of them.

Darien's stomach clenched with nervousness. For a moment she wondered if, despite her brave words, she wasn't making a huge mistake by going on this dangerous quest. She remembered how running from Grisha and fighting the charlots had made her feel weak and helpless, not brave at all. She reminded herself that this was really real, not an adventure from a book.

And she thought about how shocked her parents would be to see what she was doing. All the danger aside, they would never approve, even if she was trying to stand up for what was right.

A memory came back to her from the school playground the previous year. Darien had been sitting in her usual spot behind the big oak tree, absorbed in a new book, when she heard two older girls picking on her friend Holly. Because her parents didn't have a lot of money, Holly was often the target of teasing: her clothes were usually secondhand, her hair was cut (a little crookedly) by her mother, and it was rumored that she didn't even have a television at her house, though that wasn't actually true. By the time Darien tuned in to what was going on, Holly's hands were clenched at her sides and she was weakly trying to tell the girls to leave her alone. Darien set her book down, intending to help, when her mother's voice called in her head.

"Don't make waves, Darien," the voice said. "Don't cause any trouble at school, Darien. We expect you to behave, Darien."

She sat still, undecided and torn. When she heard her friend begin to cry, Darien chose to help in spite of her mother's voice, but by then it was too late and the older girls had walked away. She went to Holly's side, and they hid in the bathroom to talk until the end of recess, but it bothered Darien that she had not stood up for her friend.

Later she had tried to explain to her parents what had happened.

"You did the right thing by staying out of it," her mother said. "You don't need to be associating with any troublemakers."

"But you don't understand—"

"Your mother's right, Darien," her father said. "You need to let the teachers handle these things; that's part of what they're there for. Besides, you should be worrying about your schoolwork, not these other kids."

Darien had spent the next few days preoccupied and more confused than ever. All she knew for sure was that she felt guilty whenever she saw Holly, and it strained their friendship. It came as a relief when later that year Holly's parents transferred her to a different school.

Darien's parents' words still tugged at her conscience. But now when she closed her eyes and pictured herself waiting alone in such a strange place, doing nothing like she had before, waiting for Amani to fight his hardest and still probably be captured or even killed, waiting for his parents to be killed, too, while she sat on the side, she gathered up all her courage and decided the only option was to stick with her friend.

"How high can you fly?" Darien asked. "I have an idea."

* * *

From a great height, Amani and Darien circled in the sky. They knew they had just passed far overhead the massive opening to the underground mines of Mount Garddrock, but they were so high they could barely see the small groups of people coming and going or gathering to trade just beyond the watchful eyes of King Nevin Radburn and his guards. Hoping they wouldn't be noticed, Amani began rapidly descending toward the barren hills beyond the gates.

"Please be really careful," Darien said as she gripped Amani's back. It was hard for her to believe that in just a few moments they would separate, each to face their own perilous journey alone. Darien forced herself to focus solely on her immediate task, instead of being overwhelmed by the unknown dangers sure to follow. She flattened herself as close to Amani as possible and knew the time had come to begin her part of the quest. Amani's wings caught the air and they landed easily. Darien slid off the dragon's back and started scrambling for cover, even though it was unlikely anyone at the gates would see them yet.

"Go, go!" Amani urged. He made as if to take off again, but then paused to rip a loose brown scale as large as Darien's hand from his side. "Take this—use it only in an emergency. Kala's luck be with you!" Amani said and rocketed into the sky. He flew as fast as possible to get away from Darien's position so no one would have any reason to link them together, since their plan depended on Darien being able to enter the city unnoticed.

Darien hid behind scarce rocky cover until she could see that Amani was far enough away. She whipped off her shoes and tights, wincing as sharp stones jabbed into the soles of her feet, then scooped up the scale Amani left for her and wondered what to do next. There weren't any pockets in her simple dress so she finally decided to hide the scale inside her shoe and wrap the shoes into a tight bundle, using her tights to hold everything together. It was fortunate that the scale was flexible since she had to curl it around to get it to fit.

By the time she was done, Darien began to hear shouts from the people near the gates and knew that Amani had been spotted, just as they had planned. She began to make her way toward the gates, still careful not to be seen and hoping that during the commotion over the dragon's arrival she could walk unobserved into the underground city.

Darien picked her way cautiously down the side of the mountain. Amani had reassured her that it was doubtful anyone would ever suspect a human child would be helping a dragon or that the dragon would be accepting such help. In fact, he didn't think getting in would even be a problem; it would be getting out with his parents free that would, of course, be the most difficult part. Despite that, Darien thought her timing had to be just right, when people would be coming out to see or chase the dragon but they weren't organized enough to notice her or be on their guard yet.

Now the critical time was upon her; Amani dove toward the gates, bellowing an incredible angry roar, sending most of the people who were outside running for safety. A group of large, leathery-skinned animals that vaguely resembled oxen were being hastily herded into a covered pen on the opposite side of the gate from where Darien watched, the herdsmen frantically shouting and pushing against the beasts' massive hindquarters.

At the last moment, Amani pulled out of his attack and retreated to the sky. Darien knew he would come around again, and so she prepared to move. On the second attack, a group of guards in shabby purple tunics ran to engage the dragon and try to capture him with large nets, while the people ducking for safety scurried for the gates. Darien emerged from her hiding place and walked briskly toward the people. Everyone's attention was focused completely on either the gates or the dragon. In the confusion, nobody noticed one small girl slipping in from the hills.

When Darien got close enough to the swarm of people, she began to run toward the gates and pretended to look fearfully over her shoulder at Amani. When she saw he was still safe, she looked back at the gates but gave a little wave above her head, the signal to Amani that she was all right and he was free to cut off his feigned assault as soon as he could.

Darien now took a closer look at the enormous metal gates rising up in front of her. It was harder to see now that there were more and more people jostling to get inside, but from what she could see there weren't any guards posted, nor were the others being stopped or questioned. Amani had told her there wouldn't be any kind of entry restriction or identification required of her, but of course they hadn't known for sure. He did say that there would be no protection from the king's guards if they chose to question her, so she would have to do her best to blend in with the crowds once she reached the city.

As Darien passed through the gates, a hundred questions flooded into her head. She wondered where to go, how she would find her way to the captive dragons, how she would blend in with the others when she didn't know a thing about their world. She couldn't even begin to think of a cover story for herself. Suddenly, all the unfamiliar sights, sounds, and people overwhelmed Darien, making her feel dizzy and lightheaded. She stumbled and would have fallen if not for the woman walking behind her. The stranger pulled Darien out of the current of people and led her to the side of the cavern where there was a large wooden drum of water.

The rather plain-looking woman helped Darien sit against the cool wall and she wet a tan scarf from her waistband using a spigot on the side of the drum.

After a few moments with the cool cloth against her face and neck, Darien's head cleared enough to apologize for nearly tripping the woman. Darien wondered if she was going to be put on the spot so soon and the woman was going to expect an explanation from her.

"Don't feel bad," the woman said as she stood up to leave. "It happens to a lot of people when they come in from the dry heat outside. Rest, and take a drink of water. You'll be fine in a few minutes."

Inwardly, Darien breathed a sigh of relief. She thanked the woman and offered to give the scarf back, but the woman waved it away.

"Keep it," she said. "It's just an old rag."

It's an old rag to you, Darien thought, *but it might be just what I need to help disguise myself.* The woman began to walk away, then turned back with a slight frown on her face.

"Are you going to be all right here? You're not alone are you?" she asked, with just a hint of suspicion.

"Oh, no," Darien answered. "I mean, I'm not alone. My family will be along soon." She attempted a reassuring smile and hoped she wouldn't need to give any more details. The woman must have believed her because she smiled back, then walked on her way, disappearing quickly in the throng of people still coming in.

Luckily, nobody else seemed to give Darien a second look. She took a few minutes to take a deep drink of the mineral-tasting water and focus her thoughts. As she rested, she watched the passing people and tried to study how they looked. It was definitely a good idea that she had removed her tights and shoes. None of the women wore any type of leggings or pants, only dresses or skirts of all different lengths. Most wore brown shoes on their feet, either soft moccasins or thin-soled sandals, so Darien's black buckled shoes would have looked clearly out of place. She was luckier that her muted green dress blended better with the washed-out colors and earth tones of the women's dresses, although the cotton of her dress seemed softer and finer than the coarse weave of the others. And while many of the women wore their hair up under wrapped scarves or in complicated twists, Darien judged it would be good enough to do a quick braid and tie it up with her headband.

With her hair arranged as well as she could without a mirror (it was a good thing Kari had taught her how to french-braid last year during study hall) and the damp cast-off rag draped over her shoulders like a shawl, Darien moved into the thinning group of people traveling into the city. She felt a twist of fear in her stomach as she saw more and more people headed out of the city carrying weapons, but she forced herself to stay focused on her own daunting task.

The Twisted Man

Time was hard to judge in the underground city. There was almost no natural daylight; the city was lit by long curving tubes attached to the walls and ceiling that glowed with different colors. At first Darien thought these were a kind of neon, but upon closer inspection she found they contained a shimmery liquid and billions of tiny, luminescent, fishlike creatures with odd faces and bulging eyes. The glowing fish from the bright orange tube crowded together 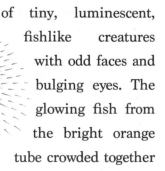 to look at her with their protruding gazes but scattered and went back to their slow swimming when she turned away.

The noise from the crowd and vendors was an endless low roar that never seemed to change, giving no clues as to when regular mealtimes might be occurring.

Darien had no idea how long she had already wandered through the enormous street-fair area, but her stomach was telling her that, regular mealtime or not, she was hungry.

Unfortunately, though the people of Garddington were free with their water supply, they were very careful with their money and food. At first, Darien just roamed from booth to booth, trying to identify what food each was selling, but the more she smelled the exotic scents, the hungrier she got.

The obvious problem was that she had no money. She certainly wasn't desperate enough to pull out the dragon scale yet, especially since she didn't have any idea how much it might be worth; it might buy an apple or a whole fruit stand. Also, none of the other people appeared to be using scales as currency; they were using gold coins of various sizes to pay for their goods. To her frustration, Darien couldn't find even one coin left lying on the ground, no matter how hard she looked. She knew that she might have to begin asking for food if she had to stay in this place for long, but it didn't seem like a very good option since she hadn't seen any other people begging for either food or money, at least here in the open marketplace. She wondered if there might even be a law against it.

Soon Darien realized she didn't have the luxury of being picky about these unfamiliar foods—she would need to eat whatever she could get. She tried to ask a few times for a sample taste from the vendors, but they all firmly turned her away, and she quit asking before she aroused suspicion. She started casually hanging around families and younger people who were willing to let her try bites here and there, but it was a lot of work for not much food, and it was awkward asking for food from strangers.

In the end, Darien was most successful simply slipping in when the patrons walked away from the stone benches where they ate, often leaving behind an oily paper wrapper and a piece of whatever they had been eating. It was unpleasant to be eating other people's leftovers, and the food tasted rather spicier than Darien liked, but at last she had some luck when a family with two young children left almost an entire wrap filled with some kind of roasted vegetables. Despite the heat of the spices, she still had to force herself to savor the food and not stuff it all down in three messy bites. *No wonder the kids didn't want this*, Darien thought, puffing her breath out and wishing she had time to go back for one more drink of water.

The one benefit of Darien's long search for her supper was how much she was able to learn about her new surroundings just by listening to the conversations around her. No one seemed to be aware of the lone girl keeping her head down and her ears open. From the bits and pieces she overheard, she found out that if she traveled beyond the food market she would find a tent city for visitors and then a loading area with carts to transport people and goods. Further in toward the heart of the mountain, if she somehow gained entrance, was the royal palace, located on a rocky island in an underground lake. Darien was excited to hear that she might be able to travel to the palace in a comfortable cart, until she also heard people grumbling that they were hard wooden carts with no seats and one had to pay to ride. Disappointed, she kept listening for information that might help her and hoped an opportunity would come her way soon.

Over and over, Darien heard the vendors talking about getting their food ready for delivery to the palace. When she heard a trio of rough looking men talking in low voices about this night's spectacle of the "giant lizards," she knew she had to find a way into one of the food carts. (The king would have had the men killed outright, had he known how careless they were being with their gossip, but Darien didn't know that.) She was momentarily relieved to confirm that Amani's parents were still alive at least, but she knew she would have to hurry and watch for every opportunity to make it into the palace unnoticed.

Darien began by observing the food vendors. Most were still occupied serving customers, but a few had started setting food aside in large crates, and these Darien watched intently. Soon those vendors closed up their booths, and more of the others started the packing process. The moment she saw the first vendor take a crate and leave his booth, Darien followed.

The rapid beating of her heart pounded in Darien's ears as she frantically tried to follow the man through the noisy crowd. He was tall but not extremely so, his clothes were in the same drab, rumpled state as everyone else's, and if he hadn't had a ponytail of such red hair Darien might easily have lost him. The farther they went, however, the more the mass of people began to thin out. So as hard as it had been to keep track of him through the busy marketplace, it became just as hard to stay with him after they reached the rows of temporary residential tents, because Darien could no longer blend with the crowd. But the man seemed focused on carrying his heavy load and didn't notice the girl quietly trailing him.

Darien had little time to take in any of her surroundings as she tried to keep up. The tents she passed were all the same light color and rectangular style. She did her best to observe little details along the way to help her find her way back, should she need them; one had a silky blue flag on top, another had a colorfully woven mat in front of the door, and yet another had a line of small metal flowers bordering the property.

Looking up, Darien saw that two higher levels along the cave wall appeared to house the permanent residents of Garddington. Each cave opening on the middle level was covered with more of the canvas tent material, with only a tied flap as a door, whereas the top-level caves had sturdy doors made of either wood or metal, all of them plain and practical rather than ornamental.

Soon Darien began to worry how long she would have to follow the man through this strange outer city. Already her feet were sore from walking barefoot on the hard stony ground, and the rows of similar tents seemed never to end.

To her relief, she finally passed the last tent. Darien slowed her pace, rightly assuming that they were approaching the food carts she had heard about.

For the first time, Darien had an unobstructed view of the terrain beyond the outer city. From where she stood, she could see that the path she was on widened and led to the line of carts she had expected to see. The left side met with the carved-out wall of the mountain. The right side dropped off sharply to a murky, still lake.

Faintly visible in the distance was the palace of King Radburn, looming over the small rocky island on which it was built. Few details could be seen from such a distance; even so, anyone could tell that the palace had been built much more for strength rather than for beauty. Its four high towers and thick stone walls gave the immediate impression that outsiders were unwelcome and attack would be impossible. *I always thought castles were cool, but that place is just ugly,* Darien thought. *I guess I'm not in a fairy tale, after all.*

In the time that Darien had been in the city, she had been both lucky and smart in making her way so far and avoiding suspicion. But as the red-haired man stopped to the right of one of the many waiting carts and set down his heavy load, Darien realized too late that she had made a big mistake in following the first vendor to leave the marketplace. For here there was no bustling crowd to camouflage her, not even a family or group of vendors was in sight.

Almost paralyzed with the uncertainty of what to do next, Darien watched from the shadows as the man stretched his back and then hoisted his crate of food up onto the cart with a loud grunt of exertion. Her only hope was that he would leave without seeing her, giving her a chance to find a hiding place before the next vendor arrived. Darien crouched down four carts behind as the man walked to the back of his cart. He didn't even spare a glance in her direction, but just as she thought he was about to leave, he came around the left side of the line of carts and headed toward her.

Frantically trying to think of a cover story, Darien held her breath. At the last moment, the man turned and walked right through the wall! Darien blinked hard at the impossibility of what her eyes had seen. She held still for a moment, knowing that if she stood up too fast her trembling legs wouldn't hold her. When she felt steadier, she approached the place where the man had disappeared. There, almost hidden by the shadows, Darien found a low arched doorway leading to a passage beyond. At first it was completely dark, then it brightened with a flickering light accompanied by soft creaking noises and slowly approaching footsteps.

The limited light still allowed Darien to see that the passageway was plain, narrow, and turned some distance ahead. A cool drift of air from inside tickled around her ankles. Remembering that time was short, Darien hurried past the entrance and turned to examine the man's cart.

The crate inside was large, but not big enough to hold a person, even if it hadn't been filled with pouches of cooked food. The rest of the cargo area was bare, with not even a blanket or a seat for Darien to hide under. In front, the cart looked similar to a bicycle that was connected with gears and pulleys to the two-wheeled cargo area in back. Hearing footsteps from the passage, Darien ran past the next two carts and slipped into another of the dark doorways. She peeked out to see the vendor returning with a wheeled pallet stacked with more crates. He began loading his cart as Darien crouched down to watch.

From her new low vantage point, she noticed something that gave her a glimmer of hope. Underneath the bottom of the cart opposite her doorway, Darien could now see that there was a long board running straight across the middle, parallel to the wheel axles. A grown man could never have fit underneath between the board and the cart bottom, and a very petite woman would have had a hard time. But Darien was only a girl, and she thought she would be able to make it work if she only had the chance to get back over to the cart without being seen.

Unfortunately, she had to wait for that chance. A second vendor was approaching from the rear of the carts while a guard was inspecting those at the head. The guard gave a quick look at the empty carts as he made his way purposefully toward the one now half filled with goods. Darien tried to keep her spirits up, but she feared that she had missed her only opportunity to make it into the cart without being noticed. She backed further into the passageway to stay out of sight, even though the intense darkness made her feel vulnerable, rather than safely hidden. She waited, feeling jumpy with impatience, but the men remained frustratingly close to her doorway.

To make matters worse, Darien seemed to hear the sound of two other distant voices drifting eerily toward her from the inner part of the passageway. She found it hard to believe that anyone would be hanging around in the pitch blackness beyond, but curiosity got the best of her and she made her way deeper into the mountain, trying to hear what the people were saying.

A young woman's voice: "There's no way they'll let you in there."

A raspy older man's voice: "Why not? They won't recognize me this way."

Woman: "The guards will take one look at you and turn you away, even if they don't know who you are. I told you, it's too late anyway. Let's just stay here until the others leave and then go back."

Man: "No! No. This is where I need to be, I feel it."

Woman: A heavy sigh. "So let's pretend you could get in. They're criminals. How do you think you can get them out this way?"

Man: "I don't."

Woman: "Would you like to tell me what you mean, or is this another one of your mysterious answers that you never explain?"

Man: "There is another way out."

Woman: "Really?" she said with a sarcastic tone. "There is another way out that no one else in the whole entire city knows about?"

Man: "Radburn knows. A few select guards know. They're not about to share the information with you. Or anyone else, for that matter. I would guess that only the most loyal and trusted people know, and even they are under penalty of death if they speak of it."

Woman: "And you know this for sure? It's really there?"

Man: "Yes. If you must know, it's how I managed to escape so many years ago."

Woman: "Aahhh . . . two mysteries unveiled in one day. I'm not sure how I'll— "

Man: "Hush! I see something."

Woman: "But you can't—"

Man: "Hush!"

There was complete silence for a few moments as the voices and Darien froze. Suddenly, there was a flare of green light, and a bony hand grabbed Darien's sore arm in an iron grip. She gasped and felt dizzy at what her eyes beheld.

Before her stood a man cloaked in black from head to toe. The hand not grasping her arm looked more like a tree branch, withered and dark, with a sparking green flame coming right out of the palm. One shoulder was hunched up and higher than the other. The parts of his face not hidden in shadow were twisted and ugly. His cheeks were lumpy, his nose was bent, and he glared at her with one black eye, while

the other was scarred and squinty.

Beyond was a sort of chilly storeroom where stacks upon stacks of crates wavered in and out of view in the dim light. Barely able to be seen crouching in the shadows next to the crates was the cloaked figure of a woman. Darien could hardly take in any of these other sights, she was so mesmerized by the disfigured man in front of her. As scared as she was by his looks, she was even more intimidated by the powerful energy emanating from him.

"Who are you? What are you doing spying on us?"

the woman hissed at Darien. The man only continued to stare intensely at her.

"I didn't mean to . . . I—I just got lost . . . I didn't know . . ." Darien stammered as she tried desperately to think of an explanation.

"Lost?" the woman demanded. "I don't think so, not here in a food cellar. Who sent you?"

"Be quiet, Jaade," the man whispered in his low hoarse voice. "I can see her."

"What?" the woman named Jaade said with disbelief. "But you're almost blind! You can barely see your hand in front of your face in full daylight."

"Yes, but the fact remains that I can see her," the man said to Jaade. He focused his attention back on Darien. "Why can I see you? Who are you? What

kind of magic do you command?" he ordered her to answer.

Before Darien could say anything, a warm amber light glowed from a vial tied around the man's neck. This unexpected surprise made him gasp.

"Jaade, look!" he cried out. When he turned to the woman, his grip on Darien relaxed and she wrenched out of his grasp.

"Wait! Come back—" the man insisted, as Darien turned and ran back through the passageway. She didn't give another thought to what might await her after leaving the storeroom. Her only wish was to get away from that frightening stare. (She might have learned much that would have been useful to her, had she not been so hasty, but that is not the way it happened.)

In any case, Darien didn't stop when she reached the doorway. She scrambled down on her hands and knees and crawled underneath the first cart she could reach, not even looking to see whether anyone was watching. She tucked her bundle in, then climbed up and wedged herself between the board and the underside of the cart, lying on her stomach. Then she buried her face in her hands and shook with the relief of escaping from the twisted man.

* * *

The cart ride was uncomfortable and tense, but it was nothing compared to the wait that preceded it. Darien had kept her head down for long minutes, nervously awaiting the sounds of yelling or raising an alarm. The sounds never came. If she had hesitated and slowed down she probably would have been spotted. Because she didn't, however, she had been able to slip past unobserved. It had also helped that the guards were busy harassing a family near the back of the line, and the increasing number of vendors were all occupied with loading their goods into the limited number of carts.

Darien had allowed herself to relax the tiniest bit, but she still felt on edge every time a pair of feet crunched past. It was at this time that her courage was at its lowest point. She felt like she was only running from one dangerous place to another, with no plan for what to do next. For the first time since being in this new place, she longed for the safety and familiarity of her own home. *I can't do this—I'm just a kid. I thought I could make a difference, but my parents were right; I should've stayed out of it. I failed at trying to get the elder dragons to help us, and now I'm stuck under this miserable cart with no way of knowing where to go or what to do to save Amani's parents. They're all depending on me, and I'm probably their last hope, but it's too much! I don't even know what I'm doing here.*

Half an hour had gone by while Darien waited, feeling discouraged and vulnerable. Her ribs were sore from lying against the hard wooden board, and her arms kept falling asleep since she had been using them to rest her head on.

Finally, the first carts had started rolling toward

the palace and Darien prepared herself to move as well. She had untied the knot in her tights, then used them to tie her shoes around her waist so her hands would be free. This time, she pushed the dragon scale deep inside the snagged leg of the tights, worried it might fall out if she left it loose in her shoe. She had also tied her inherited scarf around the board, hoping it would help her hold on if the ride was bumpy. *It would be too funny, after all the hard work it took to get here and all this time waiting, if I just bounced right out on the first big bump.*

Darien's cart had started off with a jerk, making her glad she had thought to use her scarf as a handle. She had felt, rather than seen, a single eye searching for her as the carts slowly rolled past the dark doorways. But no one had cried out any warnings about her, and soon Darien had all she could do to keep her grip on the splintery board beneath her.

Palace, Prison, and Plan

Darien's view during her difficult ride to the palace was limited to two wheels, one pair of worn boots, and a long, monotonous wall of rock. She had to squint to keep the dust out of her eyes. Although she couldn't see much, she could feel how they rumbled downward and shivered as they got nearer to the chilly lake. She could feel how they never fully turned but kept to a gradual rightward course. Cutting through the ancient, dry smell of stony dust, she could smell bitterness from the water below, causing her to wonder about the water she had drunk earlier. And she could hear how the carts groaned when they veered sharply right, carrying their cargo onto the vast wooden bridge that joined the outer and inner cities together.

Before anyone could enter the palace grounds they had to pass through another pair of metal gates set into a high stone archway. These gates were much more carefully guarded than the outer ones, and entry by outsiders was not generally permitted unless they were first interviewed, then watched over until their business at the palace was finished. One might think that the king was overly cautious, but he did have many legitimate reasons to be suspicious. Also, he knew what kind of devious plots to be suspicious of, since he had devised many himself before taking the throne.

Two guards remained on duty at the gates that day, but they watched from their high seats and never had a clue about the small girl anxiously riding under the seventh cart. On a normal day, Darien would not have been able to depart from her cart unnoticed, because usually the supply carts were accompanied to the palace by one or two additional guards. But King Radburn, cautious though he was, was also hot-tempered and impulsive, so that when he heard of the dragon's supposed attack on his city, he flew into a rage and ordered all but the most necessary guards away to hunt down the insolent beast. And so on this day, instead of the somber and methodical unloading of goods that was usual under the guards' strict inspection, the palace workers and vendors greeted one another warmly, with laughter and an atmosphere of festivity in the air.

Darien listened and waited, trying to decide whether to crawl out now and mix with the other people or continue to wait until everyone was gone. Both choices had risks of being seen, of being recognized as an outsider, of getting lost, of getting locked out—or any number of other things that Darien knew she could never even foresee. Making up her mind, she untied her scarf from the cart and crawled out on the side opposite the palace doors, thinking that if anyone saw her, she could say she had just gone under to retrieve her lost accessory. She stood up and dusted off the scarf, still putting on a show, and then arranged it over her shoulders like before, though she realized with relief that nobody had even looked her way. She retied her shoes into a bundle with her tights and tried to figure out what to do next.

Feeling it would be safer among the families and passengers rather than the vendors, Darien drifted toward the end of the line of carts. She hoped that they would not remain outside the palace long; the longer she had to stand around alone, the more suspicious it would look. Fortunately, only a few minutes passed until wide service doors were thrown open, releasing a burst of noise and intense shifting light. The vendors began hurriedly unloading their goods onto waiting handcarts to be sent off to various parts of the palace. The passengers were led by a palace official past the cargo area and skirted an enormous kitchen filled with workers, servants, food, and huge fiery ovens. Darien tagged along a few feet behind the passengers, hoping to be overlooked by them and also by the kitchen staff.

She needn't have worried about the kitchen staff or servants. Most had no particular loyalty to the king— all they wanted was to get their work done and scrape by making a living that was only slightly higher than that of the outer city dwellers. And of course, tonight they were all preoccupied creating a hastily prepared feast, though no one except for the king and his group of specialized hunters knew about the dragons and what was planned for the grand finale.

Even though King Radburn had only watched from a safe vantage point, publicly he would take most of the credit for capturing the dragons and returning triumphantly to his stronghold. The dragon hunters would grit their teeth and keep quiet, however; they would be paid generously after the dragons were slain. It was important at this time for the king to appear dominant and powerful. There were still plenty of people who suspected he had not received the kingship honestly, even if they were not openly protesting. So this would be a great opportunity for Radburn to win over many supporters who wanted to feel secure again and know their ruler was concerned about their protection. There would surely be some who would never change their minds about him, but he had a plan for them as well, one that would require stealth rather than this bold show of strength.

* * *

After leaving the kitchens, the group of passengers, with Darien trailing at a short distance, first passed through a wide corridor before spilling out into the rear of a grand hall. Darien was not the only one staring at the extravagant show of wealth all around, although after a few moments she decided it seemed overdone and gaudy. A long stone table, clearly for the king and his most important advisers and guests, stood at the far end of the hall where it was being decorated with a silky, embroidered tablecloth, elaborate candelabra, and lots of gold tableware. More modest wooden trestle tables were being added to the room by palace servants who bustled about their duties with efficiency and very little chatter. To the left, a gold statue, presumably of the king, sneered down at them from atop a stone pedestal taller than Darien. Even the walls appeared to have been painted with a twisting pattern of golden filigrees.

In contrast to the luxury around her, Darien looked down and noticed how filthy her dress had become. She saw with dismay that even more of the hem had torn, probably from her fall through the trees. *My mom is going to kill me*, she thought. *If I ever make it back home, that is.* At least the other passengers didn't look so different from her, with their homespun clothes and dust-blown skin. *They are wearing shoes though*, she thought, looking down at her scratched and dirty feet with chagrin.

Darien was abruptly brought back to her task when the tall prim man leading them began giving their instructions.

"Before any of you ask, yes, this is the Great Hall where the king will be holding his feast tonight," he said in a bored tone. "And no, you can't come unless you've been specially invited. Now, line up please and show me your mark. Once I've got you separated into groups, I can show you where to go."

Darien panicked. She had no idea what the mark was or what it was for, but she knew she clearly didn't have it. The others were grumbling and lining up to show the man their left forearms where a quarter-sized symbol had been inked.

Darien eased away from the group and tried to slip away without being noticed, but before she had gotten very far the man yelled out, "Where do you think you're going?"

"I'm so forgetful—I left my sandals in the cart," she said.

"Well, they've probably left already," he replied.

Despite his warning, Darien kept walking swiftly to the hallway. "I'll just go check anyway," she said and started lightly running. She didn't want to go back to the kitchen though, so when the man's attention was turned back to the other passengers, she veered off and slipped into another room hidden behind a thick velvety curtain, not having any idea where it would lead or where she needed to go.

Before Darien could go anywhere, she heard a couple of pairs of echoing footsteps that sounded like they were climbing rather than walking through the hallway beyond the curtain. She immediately retreated and folded herself into the excess curtain fabric, hoping it still looked normal from the outside. Darien could discern two, or possibly three, young female voices speaking quietly and coming in her direction.

"You heard the strange noises coming from down there?"

"What were they from?"

"I have no idea, but it sounded big. I couldn't see anything though; they've got the door locked up tight."

"I bet if it was Evan's turn on duty you'd get to take a peek."

"Shh . . . don't even joke about that! You know he'd get in a lot of trouble."

"You know what's even worse? The smell. I mean, it is awful. It smells like something rotten is burning. It's bad enough we have to go down there in the first place to feed those ungrateful prisoners and clean up after them, but to have to do it with that smell seeping in? Ugh!"

"And the really bad part is that tomorrow we'll probably have to clean up after whatever it is they're keeping so secret."

"I don't even want to think about—oh! Someone's coming—"

The sound of the girls' footsteps scurried away from where Darien remained hidden. She stifled a sneeze and waited in the musty curtain while heavier footsteps came and went. When all was quiet again, she peeked out and viewed her new surroundings while rubbing the dust from her itchy nose.

She had entered a wide open corridor with wooden doors leading off of it on her right side. It turned a corner about ten yards on her left. *If I guess that the sounds and smells the girl was talking about belong to the dragons, then I need to find a way to get down below,* she thought. Darien found what she needed diagonally from her position: a tall stone archway in the corner that led to a circular tower filled with a spiral stairway made of thick stone slabs. Checking that both ways were clear, she dashed over to the doorway, then hesitated. She could see that once she entered the tower there would be no place to hide if someone came along. Not seeing any other choice, Darien moved into the shadowy tower and began to carefully descend.

Before Darien even reached the bottom, she began

to wish she had put her shoes back on. The steps were gritty at first, then became slimy as she went deeper into the levels below. Soon a creeping chill began sneaking its way through her feet and up past her ankles.

The stairs circled once, twice, three times around before opening into a dimly lit room that seemed to have no other purpose other than to lead off into other rooms. It was large and L-shaped, similar to the corridor above, and had three unmarked doors leading off from it: one on each end wall and one on the left-hand interior wall. Small oil lanterns hanging from iron hooks were the only features in this room made entirely of dark, damp stone. Unsure where to go next, Darien decided to start with the door on her far left and listen at each one in turn, hoping for some clue to what lay behind them.

It was never far from her mind that someone could come along at any moment and find her completely exposed, with nowhere to hide in this barren room. She was unaware how much commotion was going on in the upper levels of the palace to ready it for the king's last-minute celebration. Because of these preparations and with many people also gone on account of Amani's attack, Darien was quite fortunate to have been able to roam the palace as freely as she had so far.

Nothing could be heard behind the first door, although Darien was unsure how much sound could

even pass through the thick wooden panels. The second door reassured her in that regard; she could hear muffled voices, but they sounded far away and she could not make out what they were saying. A low trickle of water was the only sound coming from the third door, so Darien returned to the second door in hopes of discovering more clues. This time, in addition to the voices, she noticed a slightly scorched odor drifting from the small crack under the door. She made up her mind that this was the door she would go through, but that left her with another dilemma: how to get in without being seen, when there were obviously other people inside.

She didn't have long to worry about it. As Darien listened, she suddenly heard the voices getting louder and closer. She had just a second to jump to the back side of the door before it slammed open and came inches away from smashing into her nose. She dug her fingernails into the soft wood of the door to keep it open and waited fearfully to be discovered.

The instant the door opened, two rough-sounding men scuffled through the room, pushing and arguing. From what they were saying, Darien figured that one was a guard and the other was a prisoner being taken for some kind of questioning. He was not anxious to go either, from the sound of their constant struggling. But before Darien knew it, their footsteps were tripping up the stairs, and their growling voices faded away.

Darien waited, frozen behind the door. She was afraid to move, afraid of more unexpected people. She listened carefully. She stayed that way until her hands cramped and her fingernails tore painfully away from the moist, thick grain of the wood. Darien exhaled heavily with relief after realizing that she had been holding her breath. When she felt it was safe, she came from around the door and peeked into the hallway beyond.

The first thing she saw was another door directly across from her, and she felt a thrill of anticipation that this might be the one she had been searching for. A quick glance showed her a long dark hallway to her left and small alcove on her right. A hanging lantern in the alcove illuminated a small stool and an empty mug resting on a plain wooden desk; this was probably the guard's station, Darien reasoned. She could also smell the burnt odor much more intensely now, and it seemed to be coming from straight ahead. Seeing that the hallway appeared empty, she walked to the door in front of her and reached out her hand to try the large iron knob.

"Don't bother," a man's voice murmured behind her, "it's locked, and they're not letting anyone in."

Darien was startled so much she almost screamed. She spun around and saw two dark eyes peering at her from the shadowed hallway. At first, she thought the man looking at her from behind the thick metal bars of a cell seemed rather scary and unkempt. His clothes were torn, his skin was dirty, and his cheeks were bristly with dark whiskers. But when he turned and more of the scarce light touched his eyes, Darien could see that he was mostly tired and anxious looking, not at all like many of the hard, tough men she had seen earlier working for the king.

A slight whispering sound made her realize that they weren't alone. There was a woman sitting in the corner with two children huddling on her lap. The woman was thin, with straight blond hair pulling free of its twisted style, and she wore a mask of worry even heavier than the man's. The little girl in her arms couldn't have been over a year old and the boy, who had a mottled bruise under his left eye, looked to be around four. The way they clung to their mother and looked out with such sad, haunted eyes made a shiver ripple its way down Darien's back.

"It's really important that I get through this door," Darien told the man. "Do you know how I can get in?"

"Well, unless he wants to be thrown in here with us, I'm guessing Henric has the key safely in his possession. Henric is the tall, ugly guard with the ratlike face," the man explained. "He just left with one of the other prisoners. You must've passed him on your way here."

Darien felt frustration welling up inside her. *I made it so far, and now I'm stuck again. It's not fair!* She turned her back on the imprisoned people and tried to examine the door again, in case there was a way to wiggle it open or break the lock. It wouldn't budge. She slammed her fist against it, not even caring about the loud bang that echoed down the hall or how her hand stung afterward.

The man continued to watch her with interest. "Who are you? Why do you need to get in there so badly?"

Darien hesitated, unsure whether she could trust anyone in this strange land. Then, almost without thinking, words burst out of her in a rush.

"It's a long story—some of it I can't even explain. My name is Darien. I came from a very different place and traveled a long way to get here. I'm in this city all alone and I need to save some . . . um, someone in trouble, and I'm pretty sure they're behind that door."

"Save someone?" the man's eyes lit up with excitement. "Or some*thing*? We've heard the noises (and smelled the smell, of course). Tell us what's in there."

"I'm pretty sure there are two dragons trapped in there," Darien admitted, although the man looked as if he had already suspected as much.

"I told you," the man said as he turned to the woman. To Darien, he said, "I am Will, and this is my wife, Saara. My boy here is Rian, and my baby girl is Qwinn." Darien smiled at the children, but they only looked at her impassively from the safety of their mother's arms.

"I don't mean to be rude," Darien said, "but why

are they keeping little kids in jail?"

"Good question," Saara murmured sarcastically.

Will sighed. "Ours, too, is a long story, but simply put, we owe them money that we don't have right now." A worried frown pulled down Will's brow as he told of their previous journey to the city. They had loaded up a cart full of goods to sell in the market: clothes handmade by Saara and artistically carved stools made by Will. Unexpectedly in the night, they had been attacked by a group of large, masked men who had stolen little but vandalized everything. Will's furniture had been smashed and Saara's clothes had been torn to shreds, leaving them nothing to sell. It appeared to be a random attack, but several shouts of "dragon lovers" and other insults made Will suspicious. His fears were confirmed after they were arrested for failing to pay their taxes and they were dragged through the palace to prison; they clearly heard one of the king's dragon hunters mocking them in a very distinct stuttering speech they recognized from the night of the attack. Will explained that it was true, they were opposed to the senseless slaughter of dragons, but they had done nothing against the laws.

They had also been accused of sending secret messages to King Radburn's enemies, which Will said was completely untrue. Darien noticed that for the first time Will's eyes shifted away as he spoke, and she wondered if he was indeed telling her the truth. Either way, she felt these were good people who had not deserved to be thrown in this dark, damp cell with their innocent children. Darien, resolving to help, untied her tights, reached inside, and pulled out her dragon scale, holding it out for Will to take.

"I have no idea how much this is worth, but if it will help you, you can have it," she said.

Will's kind eyes narrowed and flashed with anger. "Where did you get that?" he demanded.

"Will," Saara uttered softly as Darien took a bewildered step backward, "calm down. You don't suppose she single-handedly took down a dragon, do you? Does she look like a dragon hunter to you?"

Saara's gentle teasing calmed Will somewhat, but he still seemed on his guard. "You can't be too careful these days, Saara, you know as well as I do. A strange girl wandering around who just happens to have a dragon scale? That's worth enough to feed our family for over a month, I would bet." He turned back to Darien. "I want to trust you, but you have to tell me where you got it."

"I got it from a friend," Darien answered.

"You have a friend who goes around handing out dragon scales?" Will asked with disbelief.

"Yes, actually," Darien replied, "but it's not what you think. My friend is a dragon. His name is Amani, and it's his parents that are prisoners here. He gave the scale to me for an emergency, but to tell the truth, it hasn't been much good. I couldn't buy any food or pay for a ride here. I doubt it will help me on my way out either, if I make it that far. So if it will help you and your family, I want you to have it."

Saara came over to Will, holding Rian's hand and carrying the baby. "What do you think?" she asked her husband.

"Well, it won't get us out of here—they wouldn't accept it as payment when they know we didn't have the money to pay before. But if we could get out of here and away from the city? I would take it in a second, and we could start fresh somewhere else." Darien thrust the scale close to Will, insisting that he take it, but he still hesitated. It was Saara who finally accepted it with a look of deep gratitude and slid it into a pocket inside her tunic.

An awkward moment was interrupted by the sound of a loud thump and a stifled roar coming from behind the locked door. The next instant, all was quiet again.

Darien noticed that Rian was looking at her with something more than blank disinterest. "Are you really friends with a dragon?" he whispered.

"Uh-huh," she smiled at him. "I even got to ride him." Rian seemed speechless at this, but his eyes looked at Darien with awe. Will and Saara shared a

look of relief that their normally quiet little boy hadn't been completely damaged by their ordeal. But, with time growing short, they put their heads together with Darien's and came up with a plan to steal the keys they needed to open both the cell doors and the one they hoped would lead to Amani's parents.

Finding the King's Treasure

Saara knelt over Will as he lay bleeding on the floor.

"It's going to be all right," Darien reassured Rian as she hugged Qwinn's little body, "but don't look." Will cursed once in pain and there was a sickening crunch. Minutes later, Saara mopped up the last of the blood from her husband's broken nose with the bottom of her skirt. Will sat up and tried to get a look at his wife's swollen hand, but she brushed him away and took Qwinn from Darien's tiring arms. Rian went timidly to his father, who pulled him into a crushing hug and showed him that, other than a red puffy nose, he was going to be fine.

With a small pang of envy at the family's closeness and affection, Darien politely turned away and contemplated the rough wooden door in front of her. She lifted her shaking hand and beheld a large metal key that would, if they were lucky, open the lock barring their way.

Recent events had come about so fast they were becoming a blur in Darien's mind. She remembered the nervousness in her stomach while she waited for the guard's return to the basement.

She remembered the look of surprise on his face when he saw her in the shadows and how it had transformed into a look of greed when he saw what she held in her hands—the dragon scale.

She remembered the rush of relief she felt when Will's hands grabbed Henric by the neck, right before the guard could lunge for Darien and the scale.

She remembered how she had almost panicked when he wouldn't loosen his grip on the ring of keys, but with one final yank of both her hands she was able to rip them free. The fourth key had opened the jail cell, but by then Will's arms had weakened and the guard was able to chase Darien into the cell. She ran over to Saara, who grabbed the scale and whipped it at the guard's head. When he instinctively reached for it, Will ran at him and they struggled.

She remembered the vivid red burst of Will's blood after he received a hard elbow to his nose and how Saara almost threw the children into her, Darien's, arms. The guard slumped to the ground when Saara landed an unexpected punch to the side of his jaw, after which she placed a foot on his chest, saying, "That's for laying your hands on my son, you filthy *birmglop*."

Darien remembered glancing at Rian as he touched the tender bruise on his cheek. In a flash, Saara and Will tied the guard, gagged him, and locked him in the cell, while Darien looked after the children in the hallway.

She remembered smiling to herself as she watched Saara command Will to lie down while she gently doctored his bleeding nose.

"Wait!" Will's urgent tone brought Darien out of her fading memories and back to the task at hand.

Saara looked at him with concern. "What is it?"

"I'm not sure that going this way is best for us," he told her.

"But I just assumed that you'd want to help Darien free the dragons," she said.

"If it was just me, there'd be no question. But for you and the children to go? I'm afraid it's too risky," he said.

"Well, walking upstairs, out of the palace, off this island, and out of the city is not going to be without risks either," she reasoned. They all stood quietly for a moment, weighing their options.

Darien chewed thoughtfully on her lower lip. Something was tickling just at the edges of her mind, but she couldn't quite coax it out. *Why am I thinking of that scary twisted man in the food cellar right now?* she wondered. *What a strange time to remember. . . .* And then it came to her.

"I can't make any promises," Darien said, "but I did hear someone say that there's a secret way out. Maybe we'll find it after we go through the door." Something else was nagging at her, but she wasn't sure what, until suddenly it hit her: "Wait a minute—the dragons! Grown-up dragons are very big, so I'm sure they didn't just tiptoe past all the people in the city and squeeze down the stairs. The king's men had to bring them in somehow without being seen. And if they could get them in, we can probably get them out the same way."

"What do you think?" Saara asked Will.

After a moment's consideration, Will nodded to her. "Let's see what's behind the mystery door. And if we have the chance to help Darien along the way, all the better."

Darien smiled and was secretly glad they had chosen to come with her; it was nice to have companions again, even if they would probably go their own way before too long. She slipped the key into the lock and turned it until she felt the bolt slide back. Taking a deep breath, she put her hand on the knob and told the others, "You'd better stand back. The dragons might be angry, and there's no telling how they will react to seeing us."

They needn't have worried. To Darien's utter disappointment, the dragons were not behind this door either. With a weary sigh, she looked around at what appeared to be some kind of large workroom. Much like the other rooms, this one was rather dark, although it had many lanterns around the perimeter that were not lit. The only source of light was one larger lantern suspended from the middle of the ceiling by a heavy iron chain. Along both side walls were long work tables that held a scattering of disorganized tools and castoff heaps of wood and metal. Against the opposite wall was a black, sinister-looking machine, which Will warned them to stay away from, though none knew what it was for.

As they walked further into the room to examine its contents, Darien, her feet still bare, noticed something peculiar. This was the first room she had been in since entering the palace that had a wooden floor—strange, since the basement was damp, one would think the wood would rot very quickly. The wide planks in the middle of the room were covered by a large, thick, woven rug, worn and dirty with use. While Will picked up some metal rods from the work table and Saara tried to keep the children away from the sharp tools, Darien couldn't help staring at the rug, so ordinary and strange at the same time. Perhaps it was the touch of comfort and coziness that made it seem out of place, when everything else had seemed so hard and utilitarian.

Right in front of Darien's eyes, tiny wisps of smoke curled up out of the rug's center, and the room became filled with an eye-watering stench. In order to contain it, Will ran across the room and closed the door behind them, locking the bolt for good measure.

"Help me," Darien called to Will as she pulled on the heavy rug.

"Roll it," Saara suggested while trying to fan the smell away from the children's noses. By the time Darien got the edge started, Will returned and they easily got the rug rolled out of the way. With it gone, they could see through the slight haze of smoke that there was a large hidden door set into the floor and attached with strong iron hinges. There was no handle of any kind, but the edge opposite the hinges had a narrow lip just big enough to slip their fingers into. The moment the trapdoor pulled away from the floor, a purplish cloud of smoke puffed into the room, making them all cough and rub their eyes. It took the strength of Will and Saara working together to get the door cracked enough so Darien could jam a stool in to hold it open.

From outside the other door they heard shouting and heavy footsteps. Darien and her friends knew their time had nearly run out. Will stuck his head under the trapdoor and found a rope ladder, which he untied from its holder and began to lower to the wet floor.

Darien took a minute to yank her tights and shoes on for protection from the cold rocky ground she had glimpsed below. She gave Saara her scarf, and together they made a sling that kept Qwinn tied securely to her mother's body. And at the last moment, she searched frantically along the worktables to find something, anything, that might be useful.

"Come on, Darien!" Will beckoned with urgency. She turned to go, but then she saw a rusty old knife with a stout handle and thick blade, the whole thing only about the length of her forearm.

It'll have to do, she thought as she grabbed it off the table along with a short piece of rope. She used the rope to wrap the knife against her upper leg and then skidded over to help Saara get Rian on the ladder. Will was already a third of the way down, wanting to be the first to face whatever dangers were ahead. Darien climbed onto the ladder right after Rian, shoved the stool away, and ducked as the trapdoor slammed shut just inches from her head.

They didn't hear any sounds from the room above them yet, though they still hurried down the ladder as fast as possible. Darien was worried that Rian would hold them up, but he seemed nimble and sure of himself. It was actually Saara who was the slowest, picking her way down methodically while keeping a close eye on both children. Nevertheless, they still made good progress, and one by one they splashed into a shallow puddle of water at the bottom of the ladder.

They found themselves in a large underground cavern with wet walls and many more puddles dotting the floor. No one noticed, however, because they were riveted on the sight directly in front of them. The backs and tails of two very large dragons were toward Darien, and though she couldn't see their faces, she could tell things were not good. Their fore and rear legs were chained to the walls, and their wings were pinned cruelly against their bodies with thick rope. The dark brown one on the left began grunting and trying to turn its head enough to see them, but it was muzzled and tied down with more rope. The deep burgundy-colored dragon on the right wasn't moving at all, except for its slow quiet breathing.

The four family members stood in awe of the beasts. Darien, the only one among them to ever have been up close to a dragon, broke free and ran to help.

"Look out!" Will called as Darien dodged a brown tail aimed at her, the only part of the dragon not tied down.

"Stop it!" Darien yelled at the dragon. "We're here to help you." As she got closer to its face, she could see one eye glaring at her. Even so, the tail made no more

139

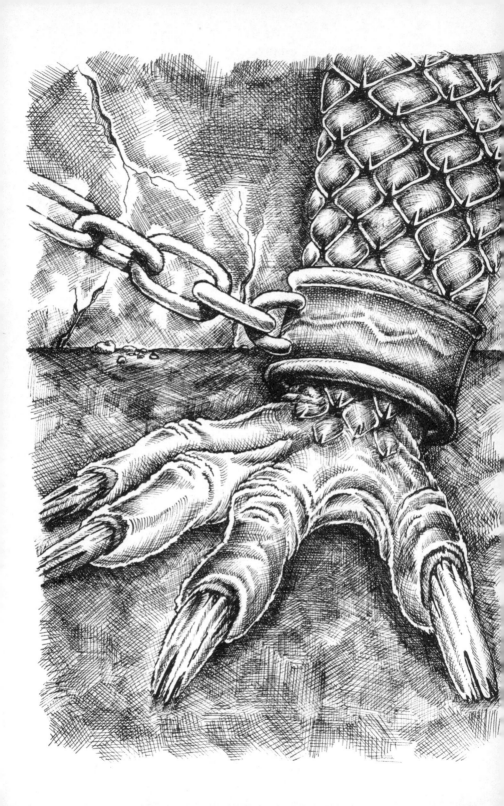

swipes in her direction, so she took that as a good sign.

Breaking free of his fascination with the dragons, Will threw Rian up onto his shoulders, piggy-back style, and grabbed Saara's arm. Running and weaving between the two dragons, they went to see what was beyond, hoping to find the way out.

"I'll come back to help, Darien," Will called as he ran by. "I promise." Darien saw Rian staring raptly at the dragon as his father ran by and heard the dragon snort in their direction.

With her heart pounding and knowing that at any time she could be caught, Darien yanked the knife from its crude holder and approached the brown dragon.

"Hurry, put your face down and I'll cut you free," she said. The dragon grunted and pulled its head away. "Please, please, trust me!" she pleaded. "Are you Audric? I came here with your son, Amani. We came to rescue you. I can tell you more, but please let me start getting the ropes off, we're almost out of time."

The dragon finally put his head where she could reach, but he still eyed her warily. She began furiously cutting and yanking on the ropes, careful not to nick the dragon, even though it was doubtful he would notice given that the knife was very dull and his hide was very tough. Every few minutes, Darien had to turn her head and discreetly cough because the dragon was still leaking smelly smoke from his nostrils. The instant the last bit of rope pulled free, the dragon cracked his huge jaws open and Darien jumped back.

It was only a quick stretch, then he snapped his mouth shut. "Go," he commanded in a deep, hoarse voice, "go to her." His eyes were focused on Brisa resting uneasily nearby. Darien didn't even think of questioning him. She ran over and headed toward Brisa's face, but Audric directed her to the leg chains instead.

Knowing her knife would be of no use, Darien grabbed the biggest rock she could find and brought it down on the linked iron. After five tries she was breathing hard, but she kept going. On the ninth hit the chain broke. With a rush of adrenaline, Darien ran to the next chain, only three left to break. This time on the fourth hit, it was the rock that broke, crumbling into sharp bits that cut painfully into her hands. Frustrated and starting to panic, Darien grabbed the first rock she saw, and with a loud yell, she smashed it down so hard that the chain shattered apart.

She calmed somewhat after that and tried to pace herself. Grabbing another handful of rocks, she came to Audric's side to work on Brisa's last two chains. Periodically, Audric would ask her questions in between trying with renewed effort to yank his own chains from the wall. Through their sporadic conversation, Audric learned that Darien had come there with Amani, how she had tried to convince others to help, and most importantly that Tabo had gotten to safety.

"Brisa, Brisa!" he urged, "You've got to wake up now. This human girl—"

"Darien," Darien interjected.

"Darien," Audric continued, "has come to help us. She said that our baby is safe. Brisa, please, you've got to wake up." His words were emphasized by a loud pounding overhead, indicating that the guards had managed to get into the workroom. Their way was blocked again, however, because the trapdoor had jammed in its frame when Darien let it slam shut.

Brisa began to stir weakly as Darien broke the final chain then started cutting at the ropes around the dragon's jaws. Up close, she had expected to feel the same heat as Amani's radiating from Brisa's body, but all she felt was a cold tremble.

"Brisa, you're almost free now," Darien encouraged her. "Let's get out of here and go back to your baby. She's so beautiful, I can't even tell you. But she needs you. You have to come see how beautiful she is." When Brisa's mouth was clear of its bindings, still she didn't speak, but her eyes filled with huge wet tears that made wavy streaks down the sides of her face. Darien wiped them away and then ran over to help work on Audric's chains.

Before she could get even one chain broken, a

brutal arm grabbed her from behind and jerked her away from Audric. Darien struggled, but the more she fought, the harder the man's arm tightened around her neck. She battled against a wave of darkness but it rushed at her too quickly, and she fell limp in the man's rough grip.

Release, Rescue, Relief

A jarring ride jolted Darien back to consciousness. She was surprised to find herself loosely strapped to Brisa's back as the dragon was running through a dark tunnel barely big enough for them to fit through. A dark figure up ahead carried a small lantern, their only source of light.

"Hey!" Darien hollered weakly. The man turned and she saw his face. It was Will! "What happened?"

Will slowed his pace to jog next to Brisa. "I went with Saara, you know, to find the way out and get the kids to safety," he told them. "We found this ancient mining tunnel. Workers must have discovered it when building the palace and realized that it went all the way to the surface of the mountain (a handy secret to have if you're an insecure ruler). I think we're still under the lake right now, feel how wet it is?" He held the lantern to the wall's edge, and they could see that it was slick with moisture. "Anyway, it just goes on and on, so at some point I let Saara go ahead with the children while I turned back, hoping to meet you on the way. Obviously, you know that you ran into trouble getting the dragons free. I made it back just in time to see one of the guards using you as a shield against Audric, who was still chained but now able to breathe fire, thanks to you. You were unconscious, so Brisa carried you out, and here we are."

"He's being modest," Brisa added. "You should've seen the way he came in swinging that metal rod. They fought, the guard's sword against the rod, but you see who is still standing."

Will's face remained hard and grim, even with this praise. "How are you feeling?"

"I'm okay—I just have a little headache," Darien dismissed his concern. "But where's Audric?" she asked, squinting into the darkness swallowing their trail.

"Once I took care of the guard and got you back safely," Will said, "Audric kept the other guards at bay using his tail and fire. He insisted we leave, and Brisa and I didn't see any other option, with more guards coming down the ladder and the dragon hunters beginning to come down a huge platform they were lowering with chains. I guess that's how they were planning to take the dragons up to the courtyard for the king's entertainment tonight."

"I never would have left him," Brisa added quietly,

"but he used the children against me. Said it would be better they have at least one parent than none. I'll never forgive him if he doesn't come back to me." They could hear the deep anguish in Brisa's voice, yet she moved on steadfastly, despite her cold, aching joints and weakened state.

"I have to go back," Darien said after a moment's thought.

"Darien, you've done more than anyone could have expected of you," Will told her. "You should be proud of yourself."

"I don't care about that!" Darien cried angrily. "They're going to kill Audric, maybe even worse now that we almost got away."

"You did your best, child," Brisa said. "Our family will forever owe you our lives. But if you want to make yourself useful, you could release me from the ropes around my wings; they're terribly painful." Darien furiously wiped away tears of frustration, then used her knife once more to free Brisa.

After a short while, Darien felt strong enough to be on her feet again, so she jogged next to Will in silence. Truth be told, riding on a dragon who is crouching and lumbering through a low tunnel was not nearly as nice as riding on one who is flying smoothly through the open air.

Before long, Darien noticed that the ground,

walls, and even the air seemed to be getting drier. They quickened their paces, hoping that it was a sign they would be reaching the exit soon. Darien's already tender feet protested each step, and even though her soles were more protected from the stony floor, her dressy mary-janes were definitely not meant for running as they rubbed and bit painfully against the back of her ankles.

They didn't reach the exit as soon as they would have liked. The tunnel kept going on, sometimes level and sometimes at a slight incline, which of course made their journey even more tiring. Now and then they passed other tunnel openings branching away that had been crudely walled up with rock. But at long last, they began to sense a hint of fresher air and the smallest lifting of the darkness around them.

Any relief they felt was short-lived. As they neared the end they could hear someone—it sounded like one of the children—screaming in either pain or fear. Will blasted ahead like a madman, reaching to unsheathe a sword he had taken from the palace guard. When Darien and Brisa reached the exit, they saw a heavy door camouflaged with rock, lit from the outside by the dying flames of a broken lantern.

Darien looked around quickly and saw Rian trying to hold Qwinn, who was the one they had heard crying. She appeared to be all right, though scared and frustrated at being away from the safety of her mother's arms. The children watched with alarm as their mother attempted to fend off two dragon hunters with her metal rod. For a moment, the men remained at a distance while Saara spun her makeshift weapon through the air. Soon the hunters got bolder, realizing they were two against one with superior weapons, and began to close in.

A third dragon hunter heaved his considerable frame up the hill and headed for the children. Darien ran to them and pulled out her rusty knife again, while Will sprinted over to Saara's aid. They could hear more men shouting and climbing toward them up the rocky hillside. Brisa stretched her wings, and though she was still too weak to fly, she was able to keep the newcomers at bay by using her tail and powerfully snapping jaws.

Saara knocked out one of her attackers, yet two more took his place. Will was disarmed, but then tackled his opponent to the ground where they rolled and wrestled and punched. Will's nose was bleeding again, although fortunately the other man seemed to be tiring.

The large hunter approached Darien and the children with a nasty snarl on his coarsely bearded face. He appeared to have no fear of Darien's small knife—indeed, it would probably do no good against the thick, black leather breastplate he wore—and came toward them with malicious determination. Not knowing what else to do, Darien scooped Qwinn up and started scrambling up the hill, Rian holding tight to the hem of her dress. Her only hope was that perhaps their youth, plus the man's tremendous weight, would give them an advantage in escaping.

It was harder to climb with the two children than Darien had expected. Qwinn's small arms grasped Darien's neck, but it was still awkward to carry her and climb at the same time. Rian gained confidence and moved into the lead, though Darien feared he would take a misstep and go sliding back down the gravelly slope. Unfortunately, it was Darien who slipped on a loose rock. As she caught herself on a skinned knee, she could hear a mean chuckle right behind her.

"Look out!" Rian warned, pointing to the sweaty man reaching for Darien's ankle. Just when she thought she would feel a rough yank on her leg, a familiar dark shadow passed close overhead, followed by a deafening roar that would have scared her, had she not recognized it. The shadow swooped back, and with one swift kick the dragon hunter was sent tumbling backward.

"Amani!" Darien screamed joyously. Amani ignored her for a moment as he surveyed the situation from the sky. He called out, and two more shadows came, pure-colored dragons flying side-by-side. In the glow

from the sputtering firelight, Darien could see that one was royal blue and the other was a dazzling shade of orange; together they helped fight the last remaining dragon hunters.

Amani was relieved to see that his mother was safe. He called out to her, "Where is Father?" Brisa sadly shook her head, and Amani roared again.

"No, it might not be too late!" Darien yelled to him. "We can go back, but time is short. C'mon!" At once, Amani spun toward her and dipped low enough for her to leap onto his shoulders. He turned wildly once in the air, then they dove straight toward the previously hidden doorway. Already rushing to reach their children, Will and Saara hollered good luck wishes as Darien and Amani flew by in a blur.

Without an instant of hesitation, Amani went from diving through the air to running through the dark tunnel. Once they were past the entrance, Darien couldn't see anything except a dim glow in Amani's wide eyes, but the dragon must have been able to see because he continued running at full speed. Darien hugged herself low to his neck for safety, and she could feel puffs of warm air go past every time Amani exhaled in a heavy panting breath. They spoke little; Amani was in a running zone and Darien didn't want to distract him, though she filled him in on what she thought he might need to know about where they were headed. Mostly she just kept her head down, and prayed that they would get to Audric in time.

The return trip to the palace was nothing compared to the earlier escape. Brisa was tough, but she had been exhausted, stiff, and sick. In contrast, Amani was smaller and fit in the tunnel more easily. He was fresher, younger, and filled with a fierce resolve to avenge the look of despair on his mother's face. Much sooner than Darien expected, Amani skidded into the cavern where Audric and Brisa had been held prisoner.

"This is the last place I saw your father," Darien said. They checked to make sure the room was empty. There wasn't a person or dragon in sight besides themselves, but they could hear the murmur of a large crowd of people somewhere close. Turning toward the noise, they discovered four heavy chains hanging down, which appeared to work as pulleys to raise a large wooden platform that was flush with the ceiling.

"That must be how they got him out!" Darien realized, pointing to the platform.

"Thank you, Darien, for everything. There's no time to express how grateful I am to you," Amani said. "But you have to get off now and go back. I will finish this alone."

"No—"

"I don't have time for your protests," Amani insisted. Darien sensed from his tone that there was no use in arguing, and so she slid dejectedly off his back. She hugged him around his neck, then backed away as he spread his wings wide. Bellowing a thunderous cry, Amani pumped his wings and shoved upwards with his thickly muscled legs. He shot straight at the platform, tucked his head, and smashed his way through, raining down chunks of broken boards. Screams of fear and surprise could be heard from above when the dragon appeared out of nowhere in a rage.

Darien covered her head until the last of the wood fell, then found herself alone yet again. She got ready to grab a lantern and make the long journey through the tunnel once more, then abruptly changed her mind. *I made it this far—I'm not going to let it end like this*, she thought. Testing one of the dangling chains, Darien found it was still intact and holding solidly to its pulley. She wasn't strong enough to shimmy up, but the links were large enough to fit her small hands, and her shoes just fit if she turned her feet sideways and sort of wedged them in. In this fashion, she was able to climb to the ceiling and see a little of the chaos that was going on above.

Darien had expected to see a main floor room of the palace, but the platform (when it had been whole) was actually intended to lift machinery, and now dragons, to a courtyard along the side of the palace. The last of the daylight was gone, but the area was amply lit with hundreds of lanterns hung from tall lampposts casting their light on a mob of spectators. There was also a high stage where the king—Darien assumed it was the king by his authoritative stature and ostentatious bejeweled gold crown—and a small group of elaborately armored men stood furiously trying to figure out what was going on.

Some of the people in the crowd were yelling at a ring of dragon hunters circling around an imprisoned dragon, and some were yelling at the free dragon, threatening overhead. Some were quietly easing away from the crowd, and others were openly fleeing. None were looking as a young girl with a dusty face and wood chips in her hair climbed out from beneath the ruined platform and maneuvered her way to the front of the crowd.

Darien couldn't hear the king bellowing orders to his dragon hunters over the noise of the crowd, but she could see they were confused and losing their order. Off to her right, she could see a small group of people harassing the closest hunters and protesting the dragon's torture. *Those people might help me*, Darien thought and headed in their direction.

In little time, the nearest hunters broke their ranks (not being disciplined soldiers but rather men-for-hire) and began pushing back against the protesters. With this diversion, Darien dashed past them and ran as fast as she could to Audric. Two hunters grabbed for her as she passed and yelled for her to stop, but they were a moment too slow. She began cutting frantically at the new ropes around Audric's jaws, happy to see that this time they had only used rope, not chains, to detain him.

Before she could get the rope cut, the hunters were

almost upon her, though Audric was doing his best to protect her with his swinging tail. Darien ducked under Audric's neck, then a searing heat burned the air nearby. As Audric shielded her, she wondered if he had somehow managed to break the rope himself. Then she was delighted to see that Amani, not Audric, was breathing his first fires to keep the hunters away.

The crowd became a panicked mob, and the dragon hunters completely broke apart. Darien was now free to slice away the ropes from Audric's jaws and start on the others holding his wings. In minutes he was free, and she asked respectfully to ride on his back.

"I will take you anywhere you want to go, Little Warrior," Audric replied. Darien laughed at this nickname and got on his broad back. Audric let out one long warning stream of fire and took off jerkily.

"I'm sorry. I'm a little sore," he apologized for the rough ride.

"It's okay, I'm used to it," Darien reassured him.

Amani joined them, but they were not out of danger yet. One group of dragon hunters, the king's most elite men, remained clustered by the edge of the stage and began using crossbows to shoot thick arrows into the air. Most of them landed harmlessly in the lake. A few glanced off the dragons' tough hides as Amani and Audric dodged side to side.

Darien tried to point them in the direction of the

main entrance, but from the air and in the dark, it was hard to tell exactly which way to go. She was squinting into the distance and almost lost her grip after Audric suddenly dipped awkwardly to the left.

Not again, she thought.

"What—oh no," Darien said as she saw one of the hunters' arrows sticking out from the dragon's side, just under his left wing joint. Dark blood oozed from the wound as Audric tried to stay in flight. Darien scooted uncomfortably over the pointy ridges on his back to take a closer look. Amani flew close and blew a small flame to help them see better.

"What should I do?" Darien asked. The sight of blood usually made her stomach woozy, but she knew she had to be strong now—Audric's life might depend on it.

"Every time I raise my wing, the arrowhead cuts at me," Audric said through clenched teeth. "If you could try to hold it still and stabilize it, that might help long enough to get us out of here."

"I'll try," Darien replied. She took a deep breath and placed her hand around the arrow and over the wound, feeling the dragon's hot blood trickling under her fingers. She couldn't hold the arrow completely still, but it seemed to ease some of Audric's discomfort, and he was able to fly almost as well as before.

"That's a little better," he said, "but we've got to

find the way out soon."

"People live in caves along the walls. Shouldn't we see some lights or something? There were glowing tubes lit up when I came through this way earlier," Darien said.

"Yes, I see them over there!" Amani called. They headed straight for the dim lights, more anxious to escape than ever.

In another few minutes they passed the edge of the lake, and just ahead Darien recognized the marketplace, where only a few booths appeared to be open.

"All right, I kind of know where we are now," Darien told them, relieved to see something familiar. "Just beyond those booths is a wide tunnel. After that we'll reach the big metal gates and be free, if they're open."

They passed over the market quickly, hearing shouts of alarm now that they were flying closer to the ground. The remaining vendors cowered under their tables and prayed their goods would not be set on fire as the dragons passed. There were still some people coming and going through the tunnel, but they cleared out of the way after Amani shot out a couple warning flames. Finding the ceiling inside uncomfortably low for flying, the two dragons tucked their wings in, causing Audric to groan in pain, and began running for the gates.

Before they could get there, they heard a loud clamor of shouting ahead of them. Now that they were so close, Amani appeared in a fever to get out, charging into the fray without slowing his pace. He seemed rashly confident in his new fire-breathing ability, and he wasn't going to let anything stand in their way.

Unbeknownst to Darien and the dragons, some of the king's guards had seen the fires earlier and, suspecting some kind of danger, were trying to get the gates closed and locked against any escape. They were having trouble of their own, however, as a small faction of protestors was fighting to keep the gates open.

The guards were getting the upper hand, but just before they could lock the gates, the two dragons (and one rider) came thundering toward them. The guards never even thought of standing their ground once they saw the fierce look in Amani's eyes. Everyone ran to get out of the way, and Amani smashed through the gates, bending the right one crookedly on its hinges.

The evening air felt fresh and invigorating. With a burst of energy, both dragons spread their wings and took flight. At the very moment that Audric thrust his wounded body into the air, Darien, who was still lying precariously across his back to stabilize the arrow, was thrown off and hit the ground hard, with the wind knocked from her. In an instant, three of the watching guards leaped out from the tunnel and were moving in fast.

I can't get a break, Darien thought. She realized with rising panic that she had lost her old knife somewhere and had nothing left to defend herself with. She had a fleeting thought of simply staying on the ground, breathing the night air and waiting for them to come take her away; her energy was almost gone. With determination, she got back up on her feet and wearily prepared to face whatever was coming next.

The guards were near enough that Darien could smell the powerful stench of their sweat as they closed in on her, grinning triumphantly at this unexpected catch. Their terrible grins turned to grimaces of fear when a jet of fire surged toward them from the sky. One guard escaped unharmed, but the other two screamed and ran back to the tunnel, their hair and beards crinkling into flame. A soft thump behind Darien told her that Amani had landed and was waiting for her to climb on his back. They indulged in just one moment, savoring the sight of the two guards dunking their heads into the barrels of drinking water.

Using the last of her strength, Darien collapsed on Amani's back and they joined Audric in their next task: reuniting with Brisa and the others. They were met within minutes, and after a little fussing by Brisa over Audric's injury, they agreed to fly together to the edge of the forest before stopping to rest.

The Gathering Place

Darien found herself smiling at her new circumstances, noting how different her return to the forest was from the journey to Mount Garddrock. Then, she and Amani had been alone and without hope of finding anyone to help. Now as she looked to her left, she saw Brisa, tired, but delighted to be back with her family. Beside her flew Audric, with Will riding on his back to hold the hastily bandaged wound. On Darien's right, Saara rode on the back of the orange dragon, Cora, with Qwinn tucked soundly asleep in her sling. Leading the way was their other new friend, Tomai, whose blue scales would've disappeared against the night sky if it hadn't been for the large, red-tinted full moon lighting their way over the barren ground. And of course, she couldn't forget about Rian, grinning and stifling his yawns as he rode in front of Darien on Amani's shoulders.

While they flew, Amani recounted the tale of how he had been joined by Cora and Tomai while he waited for some sign of his parents' and Darien's return. It turned out that although Darien thought she had been a big failure during her confrontation with the old dragon Grisha, a few of the younger dragons on the council had been impressed with her courage and her sense of justice. After hearing about her encounter, they felt Grisha had been too hasty in throwing her out the way he had and without consulting with the rest of them, though they were careful not to say this directly to his face. They had requested permission to investigate what was going on at Mount Garddrock— which Grisha granted with a scornful sneer, adding that it was their time to waste if they chose.

Cora and Tomai, new to the council and anxious to prove themselves, had volunteered to check things out. They agreed along the way that even though they hadn't discussed it with the others, they would try to help if they could. They were smart and practical enough to realize that if the king was allowed to go on hunting the exiled dragons, he might soon get tired of all the extra work required and simply attack the pure dragons where they lived. They knew he was greedy and couldn't be trusted to keep his word on their protection, which he had never officially given anyway. The stronger and more confident he grew with his dragon hunters, the more likely it would be that he wouldn't stop until he had destroyed them all, pure and mixed-color dragons alike.

When the pair had reached Mount Garddrock, they found Amani returning from a second attack on the gates. This time the guards had been better prepared, and he was looking for a place to rest, knowing it might be quite some time before Darien would return. Tomai and Cora watched for a while from a distance, then joined Amani at his hiding place high in the peaks of the mountain. He was pleasantly surprised to meet them and filled them in on everything that had happened. They agreed to wait with him and help watch for signs of Darien and his parents. The new arrivals seemed distant at first, but after talking with Amani and sympathizing with his situation, they began to warm up to each other.

After waiting a while, they decided to take turns checking the gate and the surrounding area, since their high vantage point didn't give them a direct view and they were losing light every moment that the sun dropped further down toward the horizon. Amani and Cora each went once and reported nothing unusual. When Tomai returned from surveying the land, he told them that it was becoming difficult to see the ground but that he thought he had spied a couple armed men hanging around an unremarkable spot along the hillside. Though it might be nothing, he had said, it still seemed rather strange and he suggested they should all go for a closer look.

"By the time we got there, you know of course what was happening—you and your friends were there fighting off the dragon hunters," Amani told Darien and Rian (although the boy was only half listening). "Yet another reason we have you to thank for our safe getaway."

Darien was glad it was dark so no one could see her blushing at this compliment. It made her a little embarrassed to be the center of attention, even though she had valid reasons to feel proud of herself and everything she had accomplished.

Before she had a chance to think about it further, Tomai called out that he had spotted the tree line just ahead of them.

"I think it will be safe to rest for a little while. I suggest we stop at the first clearing we can find," he said. The rest agreed, and within minutes they found a suitable place to land. It wasn't much, but the surrounding trees were close enough to provide cover, and there was a trickling end of a brook that was enough to let them wash the dust of traveling off.

They also used a little of the water to clean Audric's wound. Will and Saara examined it, and though the bleeding seemed to be under control, they said they were worried that their continued flying would make it worse. They left the arrow in until they could properly tend to the injury, but feared the increased swelling would soon lead to infection if they left it much longer.

"As far as I can tell, Audric is not injured too seriously," Will reported, "but we really need to get him in the hands of a skilled healer or it will get worse. I don't know anything about healing dragons, but I know the swelling isn't a good sign."

"So where do we find a healer?" Darien asked.

"Well, there are human healers in the settlements on the other side of Mount Garddrock, where we used to live," Will said, "but I think it would lead us too close to danger to return that way right now. Besides, it is doubtful any of them would know what to do with an injured dragon anyway."

"What we really need is to find the elves," Cora said.

"That's a *great* idea," Amani said sarcastically. "Do you know where to find them?"

"Of course not," Cora replied, sounding slightly offended at Amani's tone. "You know they all but disappeared after King Dex was gone and we dragons had our . . . ah . . . disagreement. I was just saying it because the elves had the best healers. I don't know where to find them, but sometimes *they* find *you*."

"If you believe the stories," Tomai added.

"What do you mean?" Darien asked. She was feeling a little lost. "Amani, you mentioned elves earlier, but we never got a chance to talk about them."

"Well, some claim to have encountered elves in the years since they disappeared," Tomai explained, "but their stories seem vague and the details blurry. Afterward, they could never really say where they had been or what had happened. It's as if they were not sure if they had had a real experience or if it had been only a dream."

"Don't be too quick to discount the elves," Audric said. "Brisa and I are old enough to remember when elves lived among us, though even in those days most of them were secretive and kept to themselves. They possess a powerful magic very few others in the world can understand. I have only known of two humans in my time who could equal the elves in magic; one is almost certainly dead, and the other disappeared from our land many years ago. If luck finds us, perhaps someone will sense our need and decide to help. Until then, let us be off. I am rested enough, and I know my wife is anxious to close the distance between us and our newborn child."

They all agreed and prepared to fly again. Will took one last look at Audric's wound while Darien helped Saara get back on Cora's shoulders without waking Qwinn. When they were done, Darien had to cover a laugh as she watched Rian studying Tomai. The boy was boldly looking up at the blue dragon with awe while Tomai tried to stoically ignore his admirer.

"Rian! Leave the dragon alone," Saara scolded in a loud whisper. Darien took his hand and together they settled back in with Amani. Soon the little band of travelers was high over the forest, each one secretly hoping to find help from a vanished race of mysterious people.

* * *

Time became hard to tell once again as they flew through the night sky. The moon had risen high in the sky, and they cast oddly shifting shadows on the endless sea of trees below. Qwinn had awakened with a muffled cry when they had taken off, then she fell back to sleep with the gentle motion of her dragon. Rian was less alert now, and as Darien kept an eye on him to make sure he didn't fall asleep and slip off, she too felt herself fighting not to yawn. Tomai was in the lead like before, but after a while he fell back to where Audric was slowly slipping behind the others.

"Audric," Tomai said under his breath, "we really should take a break for the night and get some rest. I know you're anxious to get back, but the young ones cannot fly all night, even if we dragons could. What do you say?"

"What you say is true," Audric said with a sigh.

"We will stop as soon as you can find a suitable place for us to land." He saw Tomai nod and fly back to the head of the group. They all began scanning the ground below, but for the moment they had little luck. They appeared to be flying over the densest heart of the forest, and even the dragons began to feel discouraged.

Audric suddenly called out in a clear, deep voice, "People of the Elvish race: Hear our need! We are weary and," he faltered for a moment, "and injured travelers. If you remember Audric, formerly of the good King Dex's guard, and friend, in times past, to the elf Macadrien, please come to our aid."

The minutes passed with no answer. They continued to fly in silence until Cora called out to Tomai, "I don't think you're leading us quite in the right direction."

"I know," Tomai replied, "but I feel as though I'm being gradually pulled off course. I wasn't sure at first—I thought maybe I was just getting tired—but now I can really feel it." Once he said it, all the dragons noticed they felt the same way, like some force was almost imperceptibly drawing them in.

Before they could discuss whether to resist the force or yield to it, the invisible pull became much stronger. The humans clutched tightly to their dragons as they all were swept into a whirling vortex. They whipped around at a terrifying speed until none of the humans could hold on any longer, though Saara wrapped her arms protectively around her disoriented child and Darien grasped Rian's wrist with both hands.

The dragons twisted and contorted strangely in the unnatural whirlwind. The more they tried to control their flight, the worse it seemed to get. Brisa, too exhausted to fight it, tucked her wings in and simply let the drafts pull her along. Finding this way much easier, she called to the others to follow her lead so they wouldn't end up with broken or torn wings.

Once she was dislodged from Amani's back, Darien thought she would feel a stomach-lurching drop like she had before, but she was surprised to find herself floating down and around the narrowing spiral. She feared that as the circles got smaller at the bottom she and her friends would race into a dizzying speed and be thrown to the ever-approaching ground, but she was surprised again when they drifted past the treetops and touched gently down in a small clearing that hadn't been visible moments earlier. She would've even kept her footing had she not been awkwardly trying to keep a hold on Rian.

With the dizzy and slightly nauseated feeling of getting off an amusement-park ride, Darien got to her feet and heard the quiet thumps of her friends joining her on the ground. Amani went from one to the other, reassuring himself that they had all made it safely. Even Qwinn wasn't crying, though she blinked drowsily around as her mother calmed her with a whispered song.

They began to regroup in the middle of the clearing when the dragons sensed something and became alert.

"Be very still and quiet," Audric whispered, his body crouched low and tense.

Darien looked where the dragons were looking but couldn't see anything in the deep shadows of the trees. Gradually, they heard a female voice singing beautifully in a different language. The words were strange, but the melody was light and friendly. As the song got louder and the singer seemed closer, they saw a shimmer in the air and felt something tingle on their skin. The little hairs rose up on Darien's arms like they were charged with static electricity. The woods began to glow with a warm, welcoming light radiating from everywhere. The moon was now hidden by patchy clouds, but with the increasing light below they could start to make out a distant village in the trees.

As they looked at it in wonder, a girl about Darien's height startled them by lightly dropping down in front of them from the trees above. When she stepped closer, they saw she was not a girl, but a small woman with lean limbs and large eyes that seemed wiser than her years, yet danced with amusement as she saw the humans and dragons regarding her.

Darien knew in an instant this had to be an elf.

The woman's hair was a thick coppery tangle entwined with braids, leaves, and vines, which swept back from her heart-shaped face. She wore no jewelry or proper clothes, though more vines and leaves wrapped her thin frame modestly. Oddly enough, the greenery that she wore appeared to still be alive, continuing to thrive even though it was not planted in any way. The elf's skin was smooth and tan, contrasting with the bright aqua blue of her eyes. Her fingers and bare toes were long and slender, her ears were slightly pointed at the tops, and her lips were the color of summer roses. Darien thought that, aside from the dragons, this was the most enchanting and interesting creature she'd ever seen.

The elf looked pleasantly at the group of dragons and humans until she saw Darien, upon which she tilted her head to the side and gave a strange, puzzled look. Audric bowed his head toward the elf, joined first by the other dragons, then the humans.

The elven maiden laughed. "Do not lower your head to me, Audric True-Heart," she said, and her voice sounded like music. "Your honor and loyalty are well-known in the elf realm. We could talk all night of your great services, but if I'm not mistaken, you're in need of healing. Follow, if you wish, and I will meet your companions on the way."

She turned and headed toward the secret village.

As she walked, the trees and plants leaned slightly toward her and she touched them with her fingertips, making them shiver faintly from their roots to the ends of their branches.

At first, their way led through a wooded part of the forest where the dragons had to follow single-file along the narrow path. The elf instructed Audric, who was first, to keep to the path, and she informed them all that they would reach the elves' gathering place very soon. Audric nodded, and the elf sprang back to meet Brisa, who was keeping a watchful eye on her husband's injured side. One by one, the elf danced through the line of dragons, speaking softly to each and, Darien noticed, touching them briefly on the side, making them tremble for an instant, just like the plants and trees did.

Darien watched the elf's every move as if entranced. The way she walked was graceful and nimble, like she was almost as light as air. She held herself confidently, yet she also seemed playful and quick to laugh. Darien saw the elf smile warmly as she met Saara and Qwinn; when she touched the child's cheek, Qwinn snuggled pleasantly back into her mother's arms and fell fast asleep. Will now carried Rian, who was struggling hard to stay awake in his new surroundings, even though he normally would have been asleep hours ago. But, like his sister, he couldn't resist the soothing touch of the elf, and he too fell asleep just before they reached the outer edges of the village.

Darien eagerly anticipated her meeting with the elf, but was disappointed when the elf became wary and coolly polite with her. She introduced herself as Kalani, and she asked Darien's name in return. But she didn't ask anything else. She noticeably avoided touching Darien. Before they could continue their conversation, Audric called out that their way was blocked, so Kalani excused herself and skipped away to the front of the line.

Darien stood next to Will feeling weary and despondent. She couldn't see anything ahead that was in the way, and her patience was wearing thin. In addition to being tired, she was also very hungry—not surprising, considering how little she had eaten that day. Fortunately, it only took a minute for the dragons to begin entering the village, and Darien grew hopeful of some rest and food. *These elves better eat something more than dewdrops and flower petals*, she thought.

Soon enough she could see what had held them up. Surrounding the gathering place, as Kalani had called it, was an enormous dome-shaped membrane that was clear except for the same transparent swirling colors as a soap bubble. The big difference was this one was incredibly strong, bending slightly at a strong push but impossible to break.

Kalani was hanging upside-down from a branch and holding the invisible edge of the bubble up like a heavy curtain while the dragons passed below. Darien hesitated at the last minute before entering, wondering whether they would let her in, but the elf continued holding the bubble to allow Darien to pass through. With a quick twist, Kalani dropped from the tree, landing nimbly on her green-stained feet, and let the bubble fall back to the ground, sealing them in.

Before Darien could fully take in the wonders of the elf village, they were approached by another elf who looked almost exactly like a male version of Kalani. Darien wondered if all the elves looked so much alike until he introduced himself as Kalani's twin brother, Kalob. He welcomed them and made a curious gesture, first forming a circle with his two hands, then gracefully sweeping his arms wide open.

He led them to the center of the gathering place where they found a blazing fire ready for them and more elves arriving with bowls full of food and drinks. The largest bowls, meant for the dragons of course, looked like cooking pots and required three elves each to carry them.

Climbing a woven rope ladder, Kalani ascended one of the massive trees nearby and was soon lost in the maze of walkways that connected the higher limbs and dwellings above. A few moments later, she twirled back down to the ground on a vine followed by another female elf. This elf was their healer who, along with Kalani, led Audric and Brisa to another part of the village. Meanwhile, a small group of elves had brought basins of water and soft cloths for the humans. Darien gratefully washed the dust from her hands and face, while the elves showed Will and Saara to a tree house where they tucked their children in for a long peaceful night's sleep.

Darien looked with interest at the forest village and tried to wait patiently for Will and Saara to return. She was awed by the elves' style of building and how everything seemed to flow with the natural landscape. The tree houses were large and circular, surrounding the thick trunks of the trees that supported them. The outer walls of the houses were smooth and polished except where they were beautifully carved into intricate shapes. The roofs were made from giant green leaves woven together. Dangling from the tree branches were delicate metalwork lanterns surrounding crystalline orbs that glowed with a soft white light, making it seem as though there were hundreds of tiny moons dancing in the air.

Darien could feel some of the tension of her journey draining away in the tranquility of the village, though her shoulder throbbed and her legs were trembling with exhaustion. When her stomach growled out loud,

Kalob surprised her by taking her by the elbow and leading her to a large woven ottoman near the fire.

"Your sister didn't seem to want to touch me," Darien remarked.

Kalob nodded knowingly, "Yes, my sister is rare among elves. She is *valpas*, meaning a gateway for energy between living creatures and the deep energy of our planet. She gives and receives the energy through her touch, but she must also guard herself from any negative or unknown energy, as it could harm not only her but also the others she touches. We elves can all clearly see that your energy is completely different from other humans, but it cannot harm us the way it could her."

It was strange to know that she had some kind of energy the elves could see and she couldn't, but Darien felt a little better at least knowing why Kalani had acted so distant toward her. Darien looked down at herself, but couldn't see anything different, except for her disheveled clothes. She didn't have more time to muse on it, however, as the elves had started to bring over plates of the most delicious-smelling food.

Will and Saara returned and shared an ottoman next to Darien, while the remaining three dragons arranged themselves around the fire. They were joined by Kalob and another elf whose name was Hemmel. Soon after, Kalani returned to report that they had been successful removing the arrow from Audric's side and were just finishing the final steps before bandaging his wound.

Darien, Saara, and Will dug into their food as if they hadn't eaten for a week. Fully prepared for more spicy food, Darien was surprised that this food, while very flavorful, was not heavily spiced the way the market food had been. Using a pair of small metal tongs, she tasted all the fruits and vegetables on her plate, finding each one more delicious than the last. She had no trouble filling up, especially when Hemmel came around with a basket of sweet cinnamon-like spiced bread and a cup of fizzing fruit juice. It didn't take long before they were all pleasantly stuffed full, and the dragons excused themselves to go wash. (It turns out that dragons are somewhat messy eaters, but quite meticulous about cleaning up afterward.)

During the meal, the elves had listened attentively while the others shared the story of how they had come to the elf kingdom. When they were finished, Kalob asked Will and Saara what their next plans were.

Will glanced at Saara, "We haven't had a chance to talk about it, but it's clear we can't go back home safely," he said. "On the other hand, they took us with nothing except the clothes on our backs. I've been trying to figure out how I could go back to get at least a small bag of our things to start fresh somewhere new."

He squeezed a comforting arm around Saara as they shared a moment of grief over the loss of their home.

"I will take you," Tomai offered. "I know what it's like to want to protect those you love." No one except Darien noticed the way his eyes glanced toward Cora. She wondered if Cora knew how Tomai felt, whether they were too proud or too afraid to break away from the pure dragons. It made her sad to think of them having to live apart, hiding and trying to deny their true feelings.

Darien's thoughts were interrupted as Kalob addressed Will and Saara. "We can offer you a safe haven for a while until you find a new home among your kind. Saara, you and your children are welcome to stay while your husband retrieves your belongings."

Saara's eyes welled up with tears, and she thanked the elves. She started to question Will further, but he reassured her that they didn't need to figure it all out that night; they would have time to work out the details now that the elves had agreed to let them stay.

Kalob then turned to Cora and repeated his question about her future plans.

"Well," she said, "I thought about flying straight back to the elder council to report what's been going on. But considering all the dragon hunting and the possibility that the king may go totally crazy over his prizes getting away, I would like to ask if I can stay here and wait for Tomai's return." Cora's expression and actions didn't give any clues to whether she and Tomai shared the same feelings for each other, yet still Darien wondered.

The elves agreed to let Cora stay too, and Kalob turned once more to Amani. "Is it safe to assume you will be returning to your baby sister with your parents?" he asked.

Amani nodded, though he also looked questioningly at Darien. Kalani noticed and turned her attention to Darien as well, her large eyes gazing through the flickering fire at the girl now sitting nervously on her low circular seat.

"Now Darien," Kalani began, "you never really explained why you were walking alone in a faraway forest and how you came to save the baby dragon. Where are your people? Where do you come from?"

Darien squirmed inside and felt strangely intimidated by this tiny powerful elf, but then she told herself that all she had to do was be honest about what had happened. "I really don't know how I came to be here," she said. "I was in my house, in a place very different from here, and I made a painting with some magic paints. One minute I was there, looking at the picture, and the next minute I just sort of fell into . . . here. The forest anyway. Then Tabo needed help, and from then on I've barely had a chance to think about what happened—I was more worried about helping Amani and his family." Kalani looked at both of them and knew instantly that Darien was telling the truth.

"So," Darien continued, "I can't really tell you where my people are; I don't know. I don't know how to get back to them, and I don't have a clue what I'm going to do until I figure it out." Her brow wrinkled with worry as she realized the magnitude of her problem. "Honestly," Darien continued, "I am so tired right now I can barely talk. Your food was so good and so filling, and your fire is so cozy. If you let me stay for the night, I promise I will try to come up with a plan first thing in the morning."

Kalani laughed, "Of course you can stay! And don't trouble yourself over the future tonight. You deserve to rest from your long journey. I've never heard of the magical paints of which you speak, but we will do whatever we can to help you return to your home, if that is what you wish."

As though Kalani's words had power in them (and perhaps they did), Darien felt her nervousness and cares slipping away.

"But before you sleep," Kalani said, "there is something Audric and Brisa wanted me to give to you." She withdrew something shiny and gold from a small pouch and handed it to Kalob. "It is not our best work, being rather hastily and crudely made," she

said, though anyone else would say it was beautiful and flawless, "but it should serve its purpose."

Kalob brought the gold piece to Darien, and what she saw took her breath away. It looked like a coiled bracelet, but up close she could see that it was actually in the shape of a flying dragon with its mouth open. Kalob slipped it over her hand and fit it perfectly on her upper arm.

"Is this made from—?" Darien asked.

"Yes, it's pure dragon gold. There was one scale on Audric's side that couldn't be repaired, and he asked if we could make this for you. You see, it's not only pretty to look at, it has a purpose: if you are ever in need, you can breathe into the dragon's mouth, and someone from Audric's family will hear your whistle and come to your aid."

"I don't know what to say," Darien whispered. "This is so amazing." For an instant, she wondered what her parents would think of her being honored this way, but their voices in her head seemed to be silent now.

Amani smiled at her proudly. "You deserve it. You're an extraordinary young girl. I'm glad that I didn't pick you up in my teeth and throw you into the lake when I first met you."

Everyone laughed and the mood lightened. Kalani fetched some soft blankets for Will, Saara, and Darien, while Kalob brought out a twisty carved-wood instrument he called a *folute*. As he began to play, Will and Saara sat close together and enjoyed the fresh air and freedom after their captivity in the dreary palace basement. The dragons lay down by the fire and politely listened, though music was not something they usually appreciated. But Darien was entranced by it: the strange melody, the fluid way Kalob's fingers moved from one note to the next, the way the music almost got inside her and made goose bumps rise up on her arms. Darien had thought she didn't have the words before; this truly made her speechless.

Kalani came and stood next to Darien. "He's truly the one with the gift," the elf murmured. "Sometimes I think he could conquer all the world's evils just with his music." She looked with affection at her twin while they listened raptly to the harmonies he made.

After a while, Kalani began to hum along with her brother's music, and though Darien tried her best to stay awake, she felt her eyelids growing steadily heavier. In the last instant before she drifted off to sleep, Darien thought, *That's strange, I feel like I've heard this song before.*

Lost and Found

Something woolly and itchy scratched at Darien's cheek and she woke up with a jolt. For a moment, she couldn't figure out where she was, then she realized she was laying on the dark floral rug in her parents' living room.

Darien's senses seemed muffled as she looked groggily around the room. She heard the very quiet humming of Miss Millie, who glanced up from her knitting as if nothing remarkable had happened. *Is that the same song? No, it can't be*, Darien thought. She stood up to look at her painting, careful not to step too close.

She needn't have worried. The painting was still in its place on the wall, but now the colors seemed faded and aged somehow; all the vibrancy and life had gone. Darien looked closer and saw the place where she had saved Tabo (*had she really?*) but there were no signs of any dragons now, either near the lake or in the sky. She carefully peeled the tape off and knew she would have to keep this picture safe and secret.

In the following weeks, Darien would spend much of her spare time redrawing the picture over and over, but wistfully adding a family of four dragons flying overhead.

"Where is everyone?" she asked as she turned and saw through the windows that it was dark out. Her mouth was dry and her voiced seemed scratchy, as though she had been asleep for days.

"Who do you mean, dear?"

"My parents. It's dark out, and I've been gone for hours and hours . . . I think. Shouldn't they be home by now?" Darien said, confused.

"Oh no," Miss Millie reassured her, "I don't think it's even been two hours since you dozed off. It's only dark because of the storm, remember?"

Darien nodded vaguely, trying to figure it all out. Looking down at the picture in her hands, she felt a mixture of relief at being back home and sadness at leaving her friends without even having a chance to say goodbye. She wondered how they had reacted to her disappearance and what was happening to them now. She sensed piercing eyes looking her way, but when she raised her head Miss Millie seemed absorbed in her knitting once again. After a minute, Miss Millie met Darien's searching eyes and gave her a knowing look in return, though she remained silent. *Something did happen, and she knows it too*, Darien thought, *even if neither of us ever talks about it.*

Miss Millie's brisk voice cut in before Darien could ask any questions. "Shall we go eat some lunch? I'm always extra hungry on these damp, rainy days; what about you?" And before Darien could answer, the mysterious woman tapped her way down the hall and into the kitchen.

"I'll be there in a minute," Darien called and took a few moments to think about what had happened. Had it all been a dream? It had seemed so real. Her clothes were still just as clean and neat as they had been when she put them on that morning, though in the other place they had become dirty and torn. But her right shoulder was terribly sore. *Did I really fall off of a dragon while fighting strange, hairy, flying creatures?* Just thinking about the charlots made a shiver tickle its chilly fingers up her back.

She checked her arm—the dragon whistle was gone, yet there was a fading impression encircling her arm where it had been. *This doesn't make any sense.* Darien regretted losing the bracelet; it had been a very special gift and beautiful as well. It was hard for her to believe she had done all the brave things to deserve it, even if it had been a dream. *I remember so many things that happened, so clearly, and I never do that with my regular dreams.*

Darien realized that standing there thinking about it wasn't getting her any closer to knowing the answers she wanted. She headed to the kitchen, her muscles aching and the beginnings of hunger pangs in her stomach, even though it seemed like she had just eaten in the elf village. Walking through the door, she felt a comforting rush of warmth from the stove, though she was too distracted to wonder what Miss Millie might decide to make for lunch. Darien deliberately laid her painting on the table, hoping to continue their conversation, but Miss Millie sent her to wash up before eating.

With a sigh, but knowing better than to argue, Darien walked off to the bathroom. When she rinsed her hands in front of the mirror, she found herself gazing back at her own face, familiar yet different too, more confident, more grown-up. There was a new assertive look in her pale green eyes and, as impossible as it sounds, she would've sworn that she was noticeably taller. She smiled and decided she liked what she saw. She wondered if anyone else would notice but decided that it didn't really matter.

Feeling a small cramp in her arm, Darien rotated her shoulder to stretch it out and suddenly heard a clattering sound on the bathroom tile. It was the missing dragon whistle! She scooped it up with delight. Certainly she was happy to have it back, but she was even happier to have something real to prove, if only to herself, that she had really been in that other world and done amazing things. Though her heart was elated, she also felt an instinct to hide her treasure, at least until she knew if it was safe to share her secret. She wrapped it in an old beach towel and tucked it in the back of the linen closet temporarily until she could think of the best place to keep it.

Darien returned to the kitchen and smelled something that made her stomach growl longingly. By the time she fetched drinks from the refrigerator and set the table, Miss Millie had served up a big bowl of steaming buttery noodles, some leftover chicken, and sautéed vegetables in a light seasoned sauce that smelled vaguely familiar, though she couldn't have said why since the odor was different from the more bland way her mother tended to cook.

Looking wide-eyed at the noodles, Darien asked, "How did you know these are my favorite?"

Miss Millie smiled a thin mysterious smile and remained quiet, but when she sat down to eat she leaned over and whispered, "Your mom left me a note."

Darien rolled her eyes at herself, and they started to eat in a comfortable silence. After a while, Miss Millie began to ask Darien questions: What are you doing in school; What do you do for fun; Who are your friends and what are they like—the same stuff adults always seem to ask kids. Though Miss Millie was a more attentive listener than most grown-ups, and she did seem genuinely interested, Darien was starting to feel foolish for ever thinking this lady could be a witch, even if she did have a box of magical paints.

They finished cleaning up their lunch dishes, and Darien was just about to walk out of the kitchen when Miss Millie paused to pick up the painting from the end of the table. She looked at it intently for quite some time while Darien's full stomach clenched nervously.

"So, do you want to tell me what happened when you went into the painting?"

Darien smiled.

Characters

Darien (**DARE**-EE-EN) A ten-year-old girl who dreams of finding adventure and excitement

Miss Mildred (**MILL**-DRED) Darien's neighbor across the street. Also known as Miss Millie or Miss Mildew

Amani (AH-**MAH**-NEE) First-born son of Audric and Brisa

Tabo (**TAH**-BOH) New baby born of Audric and Brisa, sister to Amani

Audric (**AW**-DRICK) Former member of King Dex's guard

Brisa (**BREE**-SAH) Wife of Audric

Gallia (GAH-**LEE**-AH) Sister to Audric

Grisha (**GREE**-SHAH) Head of the Elder Council of Dragons

King Dex (**DECKS**) Former king who died under mysterious circumstances

King Nevin Radburn (**NEV**-IN **RAD**-BURN) Became the new king after King Dex's death

Will (**WILL**) Craftsman and prisoner

Saara (**SAY**-RAH) Will's wife

Rian (**RYE**-AN) Son of Will and Saara

Qwinn (**KWIN**) Daughter of Will and Saara, sister to Rian

Tomai (TOH-**MYE**) Pure-blood dragon

Cora (**KO**-RAH) Pure-blood dragon

Kalani (KAH-**LAH**-NEE) Elf maiden

Kalob (**KAY**-LOB) Twin brother of Kalani

Other great titles from Windhill Books

For young readers

Darien and the Seed of Obreget

by Jeanna Kunce

Picture books by Craig Kunce

Edrick the Inventor®
Saturday is Cleaning Day

Edrick the Inventor®
Spring is for Gardening

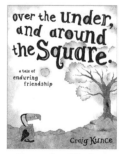

Over the Under,
and around the Square

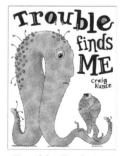

Trouble Finds ME

THE
LOST LETTERS
OF THE
PLEIAD MAGI

A B C D E F G

H I J K L M N

O P Q R S T

U V W X Y Z !